SILENT NIGHT

ANITA WALLER

BLOODHOUND
B O O K S

www.bloodhoundbooks.com

Print ISBN: 9781917705363

To Siân and Cerys, just one word,
DUCKS!

Silent night! Holy night!
All is calm, all is bright
Round yon virgin mother and child!
Holy infant, so tender and mild,
Sleep in heavenly peace!
Sleep in heavenly peace!
Silent night! Holy night!
Shepherds quake at the sight!
Glories stream from heaven afar,
Heavenly hosts sing Alleluia!
Christ the Saviour is born!
Christ the Saviour is born!
Silent night! Holy night!
Son of God, love's pure light
Radiant beams from thy Holy face
With the dawn of redeeming grace,
Jesus, Lord, at thy birth!
Jesus, Lord, at thy birth!

CHAPTER ONE

The Christmas tree had been standing at the front of the church for four weeks, and Steve Rainforth tweaked a couple of the baubles that were close to falling off. The children insisted on touching them, and he knew it was part of his remit as vicar of the parish to tidy up after their little fingers had been at work.

Christmas Eve was his favourite day of the year. He loved taking Midnight Mass, enjoyed the solemnity of it, and most of all he got to choose his favourite carols. 'Silent Night', 'In the Bleak Midwinter', 'O Holy Night' – he loved them all. The Christmas Eve service had such a different feel to any other, and it was mainly attended by his more elderly parishioners, the younger ones with children having other things to organise. It was, however, his most attended service of the year, and it gave him great joy.

He knelt at the altar rail for a few minutes, remembering in his prayers the people he knew who were ill, thinking particularly of Sarah Newbould who wasn't really expected to get through Christmas. The cancer was taking her quickly and he asked God that it would soon be over for her, to ease the pain and suffering of the lovely old lady. He said a fervent amen, then stood and rubbed his knees. It was time to check that everything was ready, the congregation would be arriving shortly.

Jenna, his wife, came through to the main part of the church from the vestry. She took his breath away, as always. Married for almost two years, he would never understand what she saw in him, a vicar of a small parish in the north of England, but she had clearly seen something she had liked.

Today she was wearing her red dress, her favourite one, the one she always said screamed 'Christmas'. She walked across, gave him a brief kiss on his cheek, and asked if everything was ready.

'It is,' Steve said. 'You had a good talk with your parents?'

'I did. They're home in St Louis now after their trip to Memphis, staying with Ben and Sandy until the New Year. They haven't opened the gifts we sent them yet, they're saving them for when they get up tomorrow, but they said to make sure to thank you.'

'Ben must be feeling better then.'

'He is. He's hoping to go back to work after Christmas, but the doctor will have the final say next week.' Ben, Jenna's much-loved brother, had written his car off in a traffic snarl up in October but was well on the road to recovery, or so he had said.

'I'm sorry we couldn't join them,' Steve mused.

'It is your busiest time of the year,' Jenna said with a smile. 'Maybe we can go over in the summer. If not, I'm going to lose my American accent in favour of a Yorkshire twang.'

'I don't think we call it a twang in Yorkshire,' he said with a laugh. 'Come on, let's get the doors open, get our congregation nice and warm, it's freezing outside.'

He placed his arm around her shoulders, and they sang 'We

Wish You a Merry Christmas' as they walked down the aisle towards the large rear doors.

Within three minutes there was half a church full of people, all chatting, wishing each other season's greetings.

At his wife's suggestion, Steve removed himself temporarily into the vestry to have a chat with God, as she phrased it. Jenna busied herself greeting the congregation, helping them settle into the pews, handing out the service sheets, and introducing herself to new faces she hadn't seen before.

The building itself was a welcoming one, with a new heating system paid for through a concerted fundraising effort by the regulars in the congregation, the ones who had turned up for every Sunday service and shivered their way through October to March each year. But now it was gloriously warm and several people removed scarves, then their coats.

There was only a couple of minutes to go to the start of the service when the last straggler slipped in through the doors and slid onto the back pew. It was the woman who had knocked on the door of the vicarage earlier.

Old Roger Carson stared at the young woman sitting a few feet away from him as if to say the back pew was his and she wasn't allowed to sit there, but the spirit of Christmas must have been upon him as he merely smiled at the pretty face at the other end of 'his' pew and mouthed *happy Christmas*.

She simply nodded in acknowledgement, dipped her head in prayer, and then sat back to wait for the vicar to come out to welcome his flock into Christmas 2024.

It was a gentle service. Steve lit the Advent candles while Marjorie Wilson played 'Silent Night' on the organ. Several members of the congregation sang along, the words to the carol so familiar to everyone.

Then Steve welcomed everyone to Midnight Mass. He let his eyes roam around, realising there were maybe six or seven people there that he hadn't seen before.

Jenna always said that the love of the Lord shone brightly from her husband, and tonight it was especially so. He kept the sermon short but powerful before leading the congregation in singing their final carol. He felt his wristwatch vibrate to indicate it was two minutes to midnight, and he turned to Marjorie. He inclined his head slightly and she rested her fingers on the organ keys before beginning to play 'Oh Come All Ye Faithful'.

The congregation rose to their feet, expectantly. Tonight was the night for the singing of the final verse, that didn't happen at any other time during the Christmas period. Steve's watch vibrated again and he knew the midnight hour was safely passed.

Their voices sang in praise, muted for the first three verses, but then their words were lifted exultantly, singing to the heavens: their saviour had been born. It was Christmas Day, time to sing the fourth verse.

> *Yea, Lord, we greet thee, born this happy morning;*
> *Jesus, to thee be glory given!*
> *Word of the Father, now in flesh appearing!*
> *O come, let us adore Him,*
> *O come, let us adore Him,*
> *O come, let us adore Him,*
> *Christ the Lord.*

Jenna joined Steve at the front as he prepared for Holy Communion. They offered each other the first wafers and sips of wine before turning to face the congregation, who had now begun to kneel at the altar rail. The queue stretched the length of the aisle, an uplifting sight at any time.

Roger Carson was escorting his fellow pew member, who had a somewhat scared look on her face, but his hand movements showed he was telling her how she should kneel at the rail with her hands down by her side rather than held out to receive the wafer. Roger seemed to have explained she could receive a blessing if she was still unconfirmed.

He stayed by the young woman's side, and eventually they were kneeling at the rail. The woman watched as Roger held his cupped palms out to receive the wafer and Steve said, 'The body of the Lord,' then the vicar's hand rested gently on her head. 'May the Lord bless you and keep you,' he said, keeping his hand in place for a few seconds before moving on to the person on her left.

She remained immobile by Roger's side until he had sipped the wine from the silver chalice, the vicar had said 'the blood of Christ', and Roger began to move. She put out a steadying arm as he had been on his knees for some time, then walked back down the aisle with him to their pew.

There was a short prayer to end the service and people began to leave, eager to get home and out of the cold frosty air. Roger wished her a happy Christmas once again, and they parted at the door after shaking the hands of both Steve and Jenna.

Jenna left Steve to lock up and hurried round the corner to the vicarage to make them a pot of tea. One last hot drink before bed, ready for an early start the following day.

Steve headed back inside the church, tidied everything away that had been used for Communion and sat quietly in the front pew for a couple of minutes. His chats with God were something he did every day, and more than that, it was something he needed to do every day.

But tonight wasn't so much of a chat, it was more of a prayer. They longed for a baby but had to accept they needed help. IVF was to start in the new year and Steve asked for God's blessing. Jenna had gone quiet on the subject, and he recognised it as a loss of hope.

Eventually he stood, bowed to the cross, and walked down the aisle to the church doors. He closed and locked them then stood in the small porch breathing in the cold fresh air. He stepped off the big stone step and turned to lock the gates behind him. He was clicking the padlock closed when he heard the noise.

A crack, followed by a thud, and ending with a scream.

Then crashing footsteps of someone or something running, but he could see nothing, see nobody.

He rattled the gates to check they were secured and turned to investigate where he thought the noises had come from. He stepped off the path into the graveyard and paused for a moment, listening carefully for any further sounds.

Nothing. Utter silence, only disturbed by the hoot of an owl. A truly silent night. He couldn't leave it, there had definitely been something, something that had ended with a scream that was almost cut short. He walked round by the huge angel statue of the Warminster family grave and moved tentatively in the darkness towards where his instinct was telling him the sounds had come from. He took out his phone and switched on the torch, then stood while he moved the light backwards and forwards, looking for anything that shouldn't be there. Could it have been a fox? They had a strange cry, but was it so strange that it could be mistaken for a human scream? It had certainly sounded like a human scream to him. He walked deeper into the darkness of the ancient graveyard, swinging his phone in an arc, wondering if he was being stupid because he had heard nothing else.

He reached what he judged to be the centre of the churchyard and stood quietly for a moment simply listening. Nothing. Not even an owl for company now.

Steve shook his head, took a deep breath and headed back towards the path, taking a more downward trajectory as he needed to go home. Jenna would be thinking something was wrong.

He was a little disoriented, not used to being among his long-dead parishioners after midnight, but the large angel had to remain on his right and he would eventually reach the path. Thirty seconds later he would be home and telling Jenna about the strange sound that could have been a fox. She would simply smile and shake her head.

He lifted his phone to switch off the torch. His battery must be doing a little scream of its own, wanting a recharge. As he lifted it, and before he closed it down, he saw it.

A leg, presumably attached to a body. He could only see the one leg but he ran towards it, jumping over graves to get to it.

He stared in horror at the sight that met him. There was blood splattered on the headstone and he reached down to feel for a pulse. Nothing. He now prayed he had enough charge in his phone to call 999.

CHAPTER TWO

S teve rang the police without losing the last dregs of his phone power, then quickly sent a text to Jenna.

Within two minutes she was running across the graveyard to reach his side. She instantly knelt to check for a pulse, her nurse training leaping to the fore. She looked up at her husband and shook her head.

'I know,' he said. 'I tried to find a pulse but I'm no expert. She was dead when I found her.'

'It's the young woman who was sitting with Roger Carson on the back pew. I don't know her name, I didn't get the chance to ask her as she arrived late. Roger seemed to be showing her the ropes because he was explaining about having a blessing in the absence of Holy Communion.'

'Of course,' Steve spoke slowly. 'I remember her now. When I give a blessing I'd normally say their Christian name, but I didn't know hers.' He pulled Jenna into his arms, holding her tightly. 'If you want to go back to the vicarage, I'll wait here until someone comes.'

She shook her head. 'No, we should both stay with her. Maybe we should open up the church hall, it's bitterly cold and we can at least make hot drinks. There's going to be police and forensic people arriving soon, I'm guessing.'

'Hang fire on that until we know what's happening. Major crimes on Christmas Day aren't that normal and they may have their own routines for such an eventuality.'

'Christmas Day,' Jenna breathed the words out slowly. 'It had moved over from Christmas Eve to Christmas Day during the service, so she did actually die on the 25th. How awful for her family. They'll never have a good Christmas ever again.'

DI Adam France was helping his wife place their nine-year-old twins' gifts under the tree when he heard his police mobile ring. He glanced at his watch. 12.23am. 'No, no, no,' he muttered, but went to find it in the hallway.

'DI France,' he said.

'Sir, report of a death, a female, at St Peter's church. Non-accidental it seems.'

'Thank you. Will you notify DS Jessop, please? Tell her I'll pick her up in five minutes. Is the body inside the church?' He knew they wouldn't be that lucky somehow.

'No, sir, it's apparently on a grave. The vicar is waiting at the site for you. His name's Reverend Steven Rainforth. Do you need anyone else from your team in attendance, sir?'

'I'll decide when I get there. I don't want to call anyone out on Christmas Day if I don't need to. Thanks for the info.'

He disconnected and turned around to find his wife holding out his backpack and coat. 'And grab gloves, a scarf and a hat,' she said. 'It's absolutely brass monkeys out there tonight.'

He grinned at her. 'No denying your Yorkshire roots, is there?'

'As if I ever would,' she retorted. 'If you're not back, I can't make William and Alfie wait for gift opening, so we'll just treat everything as if you're here and open them when they're ready. That okay?'

He pulled her into his arms and kissed her. 'I'm sorry I have such a lousy job, Elise. And I don't even want to think of what Debra's going to say. Whatever it is, it'll be preceded by a word beginning with F.'

Elise laughed. 'Debs doesn't swear, well not much anyway. Now get off and try to be back home at a reasonable hour.' She shoved him towards the door and watched as he sprayed his windscreen with de-icer before climbing inside.

She remained at the window until he had driven away, then wiped away the small tear that she wouldn't have let him see, ever. Sometimes it was hard to be strong. And a DI's wife.

DS Debra Jessop wasn't just angry, she was seething. 'Who the fuck gets themselves killed on Christmas Eve?' she demanded.

'My wife has just told me you don't swear,' he said, smiling at the stress on her face, 'but I knew she was wrong. And it's Christmas Day, not Christmas Eve. Did control get you out of bed?'

'Another five minutes and they would have done. I've left Dave in charge if I'm not back by tomorrow morning, but Kara twists him round her little finger so if she wakes up at two, she'll have him downstairs to see if Santa has been. Fortunately he has, so that job's done. But my child is a five-year-old witch, and Dave doesn't stand a chance without me there to say no.'

'We'd best crack on then and get this solved within an hour.'

He accelerated, cutting two minutes off his ETA. They pulled up outside the church, and were met by a woman standing at the small gate leading into the graveyard.

She stepped forward to greet them. 'Hello, I'm Jenna

Rainforth, Reverend Rainforth's wife. He's remained with the body, I said I would wait down here for you.'

Adam introduced them. 'DI France and DS Jessop. You have a deceased female, I understand.'

'We do, although strictly speaking we don't know who she is. She was at our Midnight Mass, came in at the last minute before the service started and sat on the back pew. She didn't seem to know anybody, although one of our congregation did look after her and help her through the Communion. Follow me and I'll hopefully get you there without breaking any legs. Please tread carefully, there's all sorts of odd gravestones scattered around. It's a very old cemetery.'

Both police officers erred on the side of caution and switched on their phone torches. They followed Jenna who seemed to know where to tread, and within a few seconds spotted the tall upright figure of her husband, who was waving to guide them.

Debra immediately dropped to her knees when they reached the body and checked for a pulse, but then looked at Adam and shook her head.

'We're the first to arrive?' Adam asked.

Steve nodded. 'You are. I'm just amazed anybody is out and about on this special night. You're on some sort of call-out rota?'

'Sort of is the right phrase. I lead Major Crimes,' Adam explained, 'so if there's a suspicious death, I get the call, no matter what day it is. Debra is my second-in-command, so I call her out.'

The noise of at least three vehicles was heard in the distance, and they all waited patiently for the forensics team to appear. Life was definitely extinct, so working on the young woman wasn't necessary. Moving her would produce a chastising glare from everyone in forensics, especially Dr

Stewart Kirkham, who liked his bodies unmoved and as nature intended.

Jenna trotted back down to the gate to escort the new arrivals and then asked if it would be okay if she returned to the vicarage. She had blood on her clothes and hands from checking if there was any sign of life in the deceased.

'Of course. Thank you for your help. We'll need a statement at some point, but that's not going to happen on Christmas Day, believe me,' Adam said before leaving them to meet forensics.

'I'm just sorry we can't tell you who she is. She's not been to this church before, or at least not while we've been here. Maybe you'll find some ID on her when she's moved. I have some things to do to get ready for the service tomorrow...'

Debra held up a hand. 'I'm sorry, Mrs Rainforth, that's not going to happen. This is now a crime scene, and until we're certain we can release it back to the general public, the graveyard and surroundings will be cordoned off, which means nobody, and that includes you and Reverend Rainforth, can enter the church.'

'Does DI France know when that will be?'

'Not yet. He's currently speaking to Dr Kirkham, but I'll explain everything when he's done. I'm so sorry, I know it's the most important day of the year...'

'Not quite,' Jenna said with a smile. 'That's Easter Sunday.'

She walked away, heading back down the path and round to the vicarage.

Adam and Stewart Kirkham walked to the tent that had been erected. Debra and the vicar turned towards them as he approached and Stewart entered the tent.

'Steve heard it happen,' Debra said. 'Although he didn't

recognise the sound initially. He actually thought the cut off scream he heard might have been a fox.'

'You hear anything else, Reverend Rainforth?'

Both Debra and Steve said, 'Steve.'

Adam nodded. 'I guess we'll be seeing a fair bit of each other, so it's easier with Christian names. And appropriate.' He smiled. 'I'm Adam. Your wife is American?'

Steve nodded. 'From St Louis. We've been married almost two years now, so her accent isn't quite as strong, and you should hear her speak with the Yorkshire dialect. She's hilarious. I hardly dare take her back to St Louis. But to get back to tonight's tragedy, I heard a sort of crack, almost like a violent slap across the face, then there was a thud that was pretty loud, all followed by a scream that sounded as though it had been cut short. It's why I thought it might have been a fox, it wasn't a long scream, as in somebody wanting help, it was short and high-pitched.' He paused as if gathering his thoughts, remembering what he had heard.

'And I was a little muddled,' he continued, 'because it sounded somewhere at the back of me; I was facing the church and padlocking our metal gates. I stood for what seemed like ages but was probably only a couple of minutes and I'm pretty sure I heard running footsteps, but again I didn't think somebody had been attacked, it could have been an animal. And apart from the hoot of an owl that was it.'

He smiled at the two officers. 'I even hummed a little of the "Silent Night" carol; it's a comforting tune and at that point it definitely was a silent night. Just to be on the safe side I went to have a look in the general direction of the noise, but even then I didn't see anything amiss until I was on my way back. That's when I saw a leg. I didn't realise I knew her until Jenna arrived and said it was the girl on the back pew. Then I remembered, because everyone but her took Holy Communion tonight. She had a blessing instead. She stood out because of that.'

'Thank you for that, Steve,' Adam said. 'I'll need all of it in statement form, but we can sort that after Christmas. I'm not anticipating quick answers to this.'

The tent flap moved and Stewart came out. In his hand he held a small black leather clutch bag. He passed it across to Adam. 'It's bagged up just in case the bastard touched it. It was underneath her body. There are cards and stuff inside it, so treat it carefully. You may have to make a house visit tonight. Her name is Lucie Barker.'

CHAPTER THREE

S teve's blank expression showed the name didn't register with him. 'You have an address? Is she a local girl?'

'She is,' the pathologist confirmed. 'I don't envy you having to make this call, Adam.'

'I'll be happy to go with you if you think it would be appropriate,' Steve said. 'It appears Christmas Day is cancelled for me, so I don't have to be up early. And I may be able to offer some comfort...'

Adam's phone pinged twice and he moved away. 'I have to call control room,' he said. He handed the evidence bag that now contained the clutch bag to Steve. 'Hold on to this for a minute. Don't let anybody touch the contents, I'll be back when I've made this call, and we can see where she lives. Thank you for the offer to go with me.'

Steve waited patiently, watching the activity around him; it was as if Christmas wasn't happening and this was a routine middle-of-the-night call out for the police officers and forensic specialists.

Adam returned, his face serious. 'Control room have had a lady ring in, a Mrs Barker, reporting her daughter hasn't returned home after going to Midnight Mass at this church. They've not said anything to her, obviously, just taken details and told her someone will be round to see her very shortly. You're sure you don't mind going with me, Steve? I just feel that as Lucie had been to the church service, it must have meant something to her. Your presence could be a welcome one. If it proves otherwise, just head back out to the car, okay?'

'Of course. I'll text Jenna and tell her what's happening while we're driving there.' He handed the clutch bag back to the policeman. 'We now have an address without having to look at this?'

'We do. I'll go find Debra, tell her what's happening and leave this with her. There's still a lot to do here, so she'll co-ordinate that until I bring you back and pick her up. I'll pop into the tent, let them know what's happening, and we'll head off.'

Steve sent a swift text to Jenna, who responded with a thumbs up and three kisses, then walked down to the parked cars with Adam, not looking forward to the visit.

The journey was short, bringing back memories of another time Steve had been involved in a death notification some years earlier. That occasion had been a child, and he'd attended because he had been the hospital chaplain – this was different. This was no half-expected death, not like little Luke's had been, and the notification had been to the estranged father.

He didn't envy Adam at all – this type of police work had to be the most difficult ever. And Lucie Barker had looked so young.

'How old was she?'

'Twenty-four.'

'I touched her head. In church. She didn't take Holy Communion, so I'm presuming she hadn't been confirmed. She had a blessing, which I rather like doing. It feels strange that I touched her a couple of hours ago, blessed her in the name of our Lord, and now she's gone. She felt... fragile, I think is the word. Delicate. Slim, long fair hair, but I didn't see her eyes. Her head was dipped the whole time she was at the altar rail. In fact, I think Roger Carson, the elderly man who helped her through the Communion, probably could describe her better than me. That's a terrible admission to have to make, but it's quite a busy service, the Christmas Mass.'

'I hope the blessing gave her some comfort. She was alone then? Didn't arrive with anyone?'

'No. I didn't see her arrive because I was in the vestry, preparing myself for the service. Jenna did, said she slipped onto the back pew, almost as if she was scared to come any further forward. And she probably was, because as far as I'm aware, this was her first visit to this church. That's actually pretty much recognised as Roger's pew, he sits there every Sunday, so he must have been quite surprised when she sat there. He did help her though, and I saw her help him to his feet after the Communion. I know he finds it hard to kneel and I've told him many times simply to stand, but he says that's not right, he kneels before his Lord. Strangely old-fashioned, but he's a nice chap. We have one or two elderly people who stand because it's simply too painful to get back up.' Steve knew he was rambling, but felt apprehensive about what was to come.

'Did you see her leave?'

'Yes. Jenna and I went immediately to the front door where we wished everyone a happy Christmas and shook their hand as they left. It was a busy few minutes because after Midnight Mass everybody's in a rush to get Christmas started, and a lot of them return for the Christmas morning service. They obviously won't be able to do that tomorrow. Today.' He shook his head. 'I'm losing my days already. Anyway, what I'm saying is that I didn't see her again until I found her body lying across that grave. I recognised her hair...'

'She still lived at home with her parents – unless she's simply visiting them for Christmas. And she walked to your church. When the mother rang to say she hadn't returned home, the girl who took the call said she was clearly upset. She'd walked towards the church with their little dog, expecting to meet Lucie about halfway, but she got to our crime scene vehicles and simply ran back home, calling it in while praying she was wrong to call it in. Lucie obviously hadn't arrived home by a different route because she still wasn't there when her mum got back. She'll be expecting our news, I fear.'

He pulled up outside a detached house on a cul-de-sac and switched off the engine.

'Ready?'

Steve nodded. 'As I'll ever be.'

The two men got out of the Astra and walked down the path. The front door opened and a woman stood in the doorway waiting for them.

'DI Adam France,' Adam said, holding up his warrant card. 'And this is...'

'Reverend Steve Rainforth,' the woman said.

Steve felt sick. 'Ange?'

He felt, rather than saw, the speed at which Adam's head turned. 'You know each other?'

'From a long time ago,' Steve spoke softly. 'I'm sorry, I didn't realise. Angela wasn't called Barker when... when we were friends. She was Angela Goldsmith.'

'You have news?' Angela was holding it together, but not very well. Her hands were trembling.

Adam sensed there was more to this relationship than just friends, but he stepped forward and Angela Barker opened her front door wide. 'Please, come in.'

'Thank you. Is someone with you, Mrs Barker?'

'No, just me and Holly, my dog, who's currently asleep in the kitchen. My husband left some time ago.' She led them into the lounge and indicated they should sit. 'Tell me,' she said. 'Have you found her? My Lucie?'

'I'm afraid we have, Mrs Barker. Is there someone we can call for you?'

'You're telling me she's dead?' There was a panic that was all too obvious in the question she asked.

'She is. Reverend Rainforth, Steve, found her in his church graveyard. He heard a noise, a strange noise, and went to see if he could find anything as he believed it was an animal that needed help. He found Lucie. It was too late to save her and he immediately called emergency services. We're looking after your daughter now, Mrs Barker.'

'No,' she breathed out the word slowly. 'No.'

'Ange,' Steve said. 'Can I do anything?'

She stared at him. 'Just don't offer me platitudes and prayers, Steve. She was my daughter, the only thing in my life worth living for, and because she attended your bloody church for a bloody Midnight Mass, she's dead. What does that make your precious God, that he would take such a beautiful person? Because she was. She didn't have an evil bone in her body, never a bad word for anyone. She certainly didn't take after her father.'

She turned away from Steve, making it a deliberate action he couldn't ignore, and spoke to Adam. 'How did she die? And who did it?'

'I don't know the answer to either of those questions, not yet. She'll be taken to the post-mortem suite where our pathologist will work until he's sure he has all the correct answers, and in the meantime we're closing down the church and the graveyard for at least two days to see if we can find anything. Did Lucie have a partner?'

'She lived here. She was about to move into her own place when I told my husband I wanted him out of our lives. It changed everything and she decided to stay. We discovered stuff about Philip, bad stuff, and she felt she needed to be here for me, and I certainly appreciated that. Since his complete disappearance, she's not mentioned moving out into her own home, although I kind of kept expecting it. Now she'll never do it. Oh God, what will I do?'

She dropped her head into her hands and Steve ached to go to her, to comfort her. Over the years of his ministry he had several parishioners who had lost children to accidents or illness, and they had been inconsolable. But to lose a child to murder was so much worse. And they had no answers for her.

Adam interrupted. 'Lucie didn't have a boyfriend?'

'Not anymore. She did have one, but it didn't last long. She met him at the time our lives changed virtually overnight and he didn't understand why she couldn't be at his beck and call every time he wanted to take her out, so she got rid of him. That was just after Philip went, so it's over a year since she last saw him. Since then it's just been the two of us, coming to terms with a different life.'

'Where did she work?'

'She has a shop. A craft shop. She was a very talented and creative person, would tackle anything, and for her twenty-first birthday Philip and I set her up in the shop. She loved it, it became her life. She ran classes, and I believe she would have completely fallen apart after Philip left without the business.' She looked up, her eyes full of tears. 'Why would anyone kill her? She was a beautiful person.'

'I promise you we will have answers. And as soon as I receive notification that you can see her, either me or my DS, a lady by the name of Debra Jessop, will organise getting you to her for a formal identification. We discovered her clutch bag underneath her, so we had her name very quickly. Are you absolutely sure we can't ring anybody for you?'

'Not on such a special night. Let's not ruin anybody else's Christmas. I have Holly, she'll comfort me tonight.' Tears were flowing steadily down Angela's face.

The two men stood. 'I shall possibly be round to see you tomorrow, depending on what we discover,' Adam said. 'I need your phone number, please.' He took out a notebook and pen and she dictated it. He handed her his card. 'If you think of anything at all, ring me.'

She nodded and followed them to the front door. Adam left first and Steve turned to say goodbye. She spoke quickly. 'Use this or don't use this, it's up to you. I married Philip three months after you and I split up, and he knew I was pregnant. He promised to bring up the baby as his own, and that's why she's called Barker. She's known since she was about eleven that Philip loved her as a dad but genetically he couldn't have children. We never had any between us. A month ago she asked who her birth father was and I told her. I'm so sorry, Steve, you found your own daughter in that graveyard. And she knew you were her biological father. It's why my lovely girl was at your service tonight.'

She closed the door, giving Steve no chance to say anything, and he staggered down the path to get in the car.

CHAPTER FOUR

S teve didn't speak. He couldn't. His mind was screaming, and he wanted to vomit. Lucie Barker was his daughter. Twenty-four years old and he had touched her just once. Never held her as a baby who needed comforting, never knew anything about her. And now he never would.

'You okay?' Adam turned to look at the silent man sitting beside him.

Steve nodded. 'I could never have foreseen Christmas Day turning out like this. And it makes it so much worse knowing I can't access the church, can't have a quiet ten minutes in front of the cross.' He turned towards Adam. 'Sorry, it's my go-to place when anything is troubling me, and the events of tonight are certainly doing that.'

'Now you're making me feel guilty. It will only be two days at the most, Steve, and you'll be able to get back in.'

Steve hesitated. He wasn't sure if Adam would be allowed to answer his questions. 'How did she die?'

'Until Stewart Kirkham confirms cause of death, I won't be able to answer that. There was blood, and quite a lot of it, but there was also a significant head wound. She was either stabbed or her head hit the gravestone a little too hard, and Stewart wouldn't commit to a positive cause of death. He wants a full post-mortem then he'll definitely know.'

'She wasn't with anybody. I'm guessing she was nervous, she arrived at the last minute, just before the service started, and slid onto the back pew. It's the position everyone takes if they have to leave in a hurry, or have to leave before our service ends – or are newcomers and not sure what to do. We have a dedicated helper who looks out for anyone attending for the first time, but she wasn't here, she's gone to her daughter's in Newcastle for Christmas. I guess that's why Roger helped Lucie. He's a bit of a grump, keeps himself to himself, but clearly spotted she needed some guidance.'

'When you heard the noise, how long was it after the church had emptied?'

Steve thought for a moment. 'I switched off all the lights, checked the vestry was secure, locked the main doors into the church and was just securing the padlock on the metal gates, so I would say ten minutes or so. She was one of the first to leave, because we shook hands with Roger, then with her, and slowly everyone drifted away. That took a good ten minutes, then ten minutes to lock up, so twenty, twenty-five minutes after the end of the service. I didn't see anyone waiting for her, didn't see which way she went. Roger said goodnight to her, and that was it. It was quite a busy few minutes. And as you saw for yourself, it's a dark little area. Whoever did this could have hidden anywhere and just waited for her to appear. Jenna was with me to wish everyone a happy Christmas as they left, so it might be worth your while speaking with her, she may have spotted something I missed.'

'Thank you, I will. But not tonight. This will be put on hold until Boxing Day. We'll be chasing our own tails trying to speak to people on Christmas Day, I fear. And I don't think my twins will be too impressed if I disappear. We've got them new bikes, so I suspect most of our Christmas Day will be spent in a park somewhere. You don't have any children?'

Steve shook his head. 'Starting IVF in February. Hopefully by this time next year I'll be a dad, or very close to being one. Jenna is getting really wound up about it, but I feel optimistic.' Again he felt sick. His calling to the clergy had cost him his daughter, but it had been Ange, not him, who had called off their relationship – she didn't want to be married to a vicar, she wanted a career of her own that was unrelated to the church.

And he had accepted that. Would he have fought to keep their love if he had found out she was pregnant? He didn't know, and it was all irrelevant because he hadn't known. He had spent years becoming a valued member of the Church of England, and ultimately meeting and falling in love with Jenna, who had wholeheartedly embraced his vocation and said yes to his proposal of marriage. And yet on his wedding day, he had thought of Ange and what could have been...

They reached the church just as the trolley bearing the body of Lucie Barker was being carefully manoeuvred across the grass and towards the path. They stood to one side, and Stewart nodded as he reached them.

Steve held up a hand. 'A small prayer?'

Both Stewart and Adam stepped away, and Steve laid his hand on the hidden form inside the black zipped-up container.

This time he knew her name. 'May the Lord bless you and keep you, Lucie. Surround her with your angels, Lord, and guide everyone towards finding who did this. I ask this in Jesus's name, amen.'

He stepped aside, and Stewart nodded towards the two

assistants, indicating they should carry on towards the mortuary vehicle. Steve hurriedly brushed his tears away and murmured the final words of his prayer once again. 'In Jesus's name, amen.'

'Amen.'

He turned around and saw DS Jessop.

'That was a lovely thing to do,' Debra said. 'She was so young, and for it to happen on such a special day in the Christian calendar, it doesn't bear thinking about. It lightened the load a little to hear you pray over her. Thank you.'

Adam had escorted the trolley down to the van and was speaking with the pathologist, where he remained until the vehicle drove away. He looked troubled as he walked back up the slight incline of the path, where Debra and Steve remained chatting.

'He's pretty certain cause of death will be exsanguination following a knife wound to the neck. It would explain the cut off scream you heard, Steve. He's starting the post-mortem on Friday the 27th, first thing, when hopefully we'll have some sort of confirmation of what happened. In the meantime, we're leaving officers on patrol here, getting search teams in on Thursday. We need to find the knife, so we'll be fingertip searching in case the killer threw it or dropped it. That's why we can't give you access to your building or your grounds. Thank goodness your vicarage is off site, at least you can be at home.'

'And there's no early rising for me if we can't have our Christmas Day service. Although I suppose I should be available at the gate to the churchyard to explain what's happening. This is one Christmas we won't forget in a hurry.'

Jenna was in bed when Steve crept quietly into the bedroom. Then he spotted the glow from her Kindle.

'Not asleep then?'

She switched off her Kindle and placed it on the bedside table. 'Couldn't sleep. The sight of that poor girl face down on a grave – it doesn't bear thinking about, yet it's all I can think about. How are her family?'

'There's only her mum. It seems her dad left some time ago, and she had no siblings. Her mum's devastated but didn't want us to call anybody. I suspect she'll hold it together until she has to identify Lucie and then she'll fall apart. It was such a beautiful Mass, and now everything feels... alien. There's no service in the morning, the church and grounds are a crime scene, so I'm going to be down at the small gate for about nine to speak to anyone who arrives expecting it, because they probably won't know about the sad events. Police officers are going to be on duty protecting the site, and they're starting a fingertip search tomorrow. Boxing Day,' he added, clarifying what day it was. His brain felt a little muddled.

'Would a hot drink help you sleep?'

Steve shook his head. 'No, I'll set my alarm for eight and cross my fingers that sleep comes quickly. After I've sorted everyone out who turns up for the Christmas morning service, maybe we can go for a walk? Clear our heads.'

'That would be lovely. The police definitely won't need us?'

'That was my understanding.' He yawned. 'Are you okay? It wasn't a good end to our favourite service, was it?' He shivered and pulled Jenna close to him. 'And it's freezing.'

'I'm fine. Trying not to picture the grave she was lying on. So much blood. And she was such a pretty girl, wasn't she?'

'She was.' He snuggled a little closer to Jenna and kissed the back of her head. His thoughts eventually burst through; he had tried to quell them for the past couple of hours. He would have to tell Jenna who Lucie Barker was in relation to him, and he had no idea how she would react. Probably with common sense, possibly with a little anger that he hadn't been given the chance to be a father to his daughter, and almost certainly with support for him. Did he deserve it? He didn't know.

He felt his wife slowly relax and drift off to sleep, but his mind wouldn't settle. He had no doubt that what Angela had told him was the absolute truth. There was no reason to say it if it hadn't been. And it seemed Lucie had known, but he was guessing that was a fairly recent piece of knowledge, brought about by her own curiosity once Philip Barker was no longer a father figure in her life. Had Angela told Lucie in a moment of weakness? Turmoil can bring on strange feelings. Maybe she had felt the need to confess. But was it connected to the death of Lucie? Or was that something else completely?

At six o'clock he got up, realising sleep wasn't going to come. He quietly left the bedroom and headed downstairs, avoiding the creaky treads on the way down. Jenna didn't need to be awake as well.

He checked the kettle had water in it and switched it on. He popped a camomile tea bag into a cup, and waited for it to infuse. The patient wait saw him eat three Rich Tea biscuits.

He sat at the kitchen table, deep in thought, and wishing today could be over. It appeared to have put a complete stop to any sort of progression with the case, and also to have put a halt to his church activities. Not a good situation, but out of his control. He sipped at his drink and absent-mindedly helped himself to a fourth biscuit.

He heard the creak of the stairs and realised Jenna had given in as well. He glanced at the clock on the wall – just after half past six – and knew they would be in bed by eight that night.

He turned and held out his arms as she came through the door. She settled on his knee and wrapped her arms around him.

'Bad night for both of us,' she whispered. 'I'll get dressed in a minute and go down to the church, see if our watch-dog policemen need a hot drink or food. It's the least I can do.'

'I'll go with you. I should be saying happy Christmas, but it doesn't feel like that, does it?'

CHAPTER FIVE

The ground was covered in frost when Jenna and Steve left the vicarage to walk around to the church. They had dressed warmly, Steve wearing his clerical garb from the previous evening as he couldn't get into the vestry for fresh garments. They had settled for thick coats, and both pulled up their hoods within a minute of leaving home.

'This frost is almost like snow,' Steve grumbled. 'The poor lads who've been on duty all night must be frozen.'

'Then let's find them and I'll nip back home if they want anything.'

They reached the gate, now closed off firmly with crime scene tape, and the two officers on duty got out of the car and walked towards them.

'Morning, Reverend,' the older man said.

'It's Steve. And we came round to see if you wanted a drink, or a bacon sandwich. Or anything! My wife makes a mean Christmas cake.'

'We'd certainly appreciate a cup of tea, the flasks we brought with us are empty now and we're not sure what time our replacements will be here.'

'Sugar and milk?' Jenna asked. 'And shall I refill your flasks in case it's a while before anybody sets you free?'

'Just milk for both of us, thanks.' He handed over two flasks. 'Thank you so much, you're a star. We've still got some sandwiches and snacks left, we came well prepared for a long shift, but the tea disappeared pretty fast. It's been a cold night.'

They watched as she walked back to the vicarage, and Steve leaned against the gate. 'Has anybody been?'

'Just a dog walker, who apparently thought he was coming later to the Christmas Day service. We had to tell him what had happened, or a limited version of it anyway, so he's gone home to ring a couple of people and ask everyone to pass it on. You may not be overwhelmed with a large group of parishioners arriving en masse.'

'Good, I had visions of having to tell the bad news repeatedly.'

'Did you know her, the young lady?'

Steve shook his head. 'No, she was at the Midnight Mass but I hadn't seen her before. She seemed a little nervous, but I suspect that was because she wasn't a regular churchgoer. It can be a bit daunting, I fear.'

'Well other than you two and that dog-walker chap, we've seen nobody since the forensic people disappeared.' The younger of the two officers finally joined in. 'It's all felt really out of kilter. It's like the world shut down because it was Christmas Eve. I suppose it will all change tomorrow because everybody will be here, ferreting around all the graves.'

'And there's only been the two of you?'

'Yep. We've taken it in turns to walk round the perimeter and it's a fair-sized property you have here. We really needed another vehicle at the back side, but it's Christmas.'

Steve smiled. 'You're right, it is Christmas. It's become somewhat strange because it's many, many years since I didn't attend a service on Christmas morning, and I'd really give anything to be leading the worship this morning.'

Only three people arrived, Virginia and Harold Walker, and Charles Broadhead. Steve gently explained the situation and said the next service would be on Sunday 29th, unless anything was found in the graveyard that might cause further delays.

Jenna remained with him, and they met the two replacement officers who arrived at nine o'clock.

At ten o'clock they decided nobody else would be coming, and they headed home to warm themselves while debating how the rest of their Christmas Day was going to pan out.

The vicarage smelt delicious.

'Turkey, it's been cooking for an hour,' Jenna explained.

'Smells gorgeous. Are we okay going out for a walk and leaving it?'

Jenna laughed. 'We are. It's on a very low heat, as is the pork. Everything else is prepped, and I'll deal with cooking it all whenever we're ready, but I feel we might need a little nap at some point. Neither of us slept last night.'

'Let's have another hot drink to fortify us, then head down into the woods. We'll not stay out too long, it's much too cold, but I think after last night we need a bit of down time anyway.'

Steve was subdued, hardly talking as they walked down the well-worn path through the local woods. He would have to make contact with Angela Barker – their thirty second covert conversation as he left her home had caused untold grief inside him for many reasons, not least of which was that if Angela had spoken the truth, he would ultimately have to tell Jenna. And with IVF looming for them in the near future, the fact he had already fathered a daughter would definitely not go down well. *If* Angela had spoken the truth... Deep down, though, he knew she wouldn't invent something like that. He could remember so much of their last conversation when she had given back his engagement ring, saying she knew she could never be a vicar's wife. He should find somebody with a stronger faith than hers and marry them.

But he had wanted Ange. Had loved her. Seeing her again had brought every good and bad memory back, and he needed a conversation with her that lasted longer than the brief doorstep exchange they'd had.

Steve and Jenna returned to the vicarage, shivering with cold. The temperature seemed to be dropping by the second, and they turned the heating up a couple of degrees before snuggling closely together on the sofa.

He could hear the drowsiness in Jenna's voice as she suggested they have a nap, and then eat about four o'clock.

'Fine by me,' he said, kissing her gently on her head. 'Alexa, set an alarm for half past two.'

'Alarm set for two thirty,' the little round ball responded.

They settled down at opposite ends of the long sofa, and within a couple of minutes Jenna's eyes had closed. Steve's hadn't.

He gently covered her with a fleece blanket and left her to sleep. He went into his office and opened up his laptop. He didn't know why he thought it might be a good idea, and he cheerfully admitted his technical skills were amateur at best, but he needed to put Angela Barker into the search engine and see if he could find anything. He would have a stab at Facebook if nothing showed up on Google.

The search brought up absolutely nothing. He tried Angela

Barker, Angela Goldsmith, Lucie Barker, and Philip Barker. It didn't appear that whatever bad actions and decisions Philip Barker had made, which resulted in his wife despatching him from their home, had made it onto the internet.

He clicked on Facebook and immediately found Angela, but he guessed the information was limited because she wasn't on his friends list. It told him the bare minimum – that her home town was Sheffield, that she had been born in Sheffield, and her date of birth was the first of April 1979. He remembered the laughter they had shared because their birth dates were the same, even to the year. April Fool's Day. It had added something unexpected and special to their relationship, but not enough to make Ange want to share his calling to the church. Her general information revealed she enjoyed watching documentaries on wildlife, and *The West Wing*, which she apparently had watched seven times in its entirety.

But that was it. He found nothing else. Philip didn't show up at all, and Lucie's offerings were very minimal. He then tried asking Google for craft shops in Sheffield, but wasn't sure he would find that helpful because he guessed craft shop owners would want their businesses to have crafty names, giving no clues as to their owners' names.

He felt a little surprised by how many were listed, and he carefully went down them hoping inspiration would strike. And it did. *LucieB for all your crafting supplies. Tuition in every craft, call now for information regarding bookings.* He quickly screenshot the page and closed down his laptop – Alexa had obliged with the pre-booked alarm call.

He heard his wife's groggy voice telling Alexa not to be so noisy, then heard her repeat 'Alexa, stop'. Steve was in the hallway by the time Jenna had surfaced from what had clearly been a deep sleep, and he held his arms out to her.

'You need some help?'

'No, everything's ready just for cooking. Go find something inspirational on TV,' she said.

'Not sure I want to watch *The Sound of Music* for the twentieth time,' he said.

''Course you do. It's about nuns.'

'I could open some wine.'

'You could. That might be a good idea, but then get out from under my feet and let me do my chef bit.' She smiled at the man she adored and would do anything for. 'Let me spoil you.'

He grinned. 'I'm up for that. And what wine? A Nuit-Saint-Georges?'

'Well, I know this makes me sound a bit of a heathen, but if it's red it tastes the same as every other red wine, so you choose. I'm sure your taste buds work very differently to mine. Then get out of my kitchen!'

He didn't bother to switch on the television, instead he simply sat in his favourite armchair and let his mind roam. A daughter. Unless Ange was lying, of course, but he couldn't think why she would do that. And Lucie had arrived at his church having never been there before; she must have had a good reason. A reason provided by the woman he had made love to and impregnated without knowing it.

He gave in after quarter of an hour of different thoughts swamping his mind, and decided to go down to the church to make sure the officers had food and drinks. It was getting colder and he didn't envy the overnight shift. It would definitely be a freezing frosty night.

One PC was inside the car, and the other was heading down the path. He waited until the ambulant one reached him, introduced himself, and asked if they had refreshments.

'We do, sir, thank you. Brought two flasks each, plenty of

sandwiches. We won't starve. It's just so cold. We've had one or two arrive with flowers, left them by the gate. Apart from that it's been quiet.'

'It'll be busier tomorrow,' Steve said. 'I understand my churchyard will be overrun by officers and forensics searching for anything they can find. And then I can get back into my church and do my job. It's been the oddest Christmas Day I've ever experienced, from a vicar's point of view.'

'You should be able to go back inside the building in time for the Sunday service. Then you'll be really busy because everybody will be asking questions and you'll have no answers for them.'

'I know. Now get back in the car and warm yourself. You're sure you don't need anything?'

'No, we're fine, and there's been nobody to speak to or anything. Thank you for asking though, and I hope this hasn't completely ruined Christmas for you and your wife.'

If only you knew, Steve thought as he lifted his hand in acknowledgement and headed back to the vicarage, where he knew Jenna would be finishing off their table in preparation for their meal. If only he felt hungry instead of devastated.

CHAPTER SIX

oxing Day proved to be even colder than Christmas Day, and by 6am Steve was overriding the automatic setting for the heating to come on, then getting back in bed to hopefully find some warmth. He dozed once again, but by seven was downstairs making pancakes for breakfast.

He carried the tray upstairs and found Jenna reading her Kindle. She looked up and smiled. 'I could tell you were making drinks, but I didn't expect breakfast in bed.'

He placed a coffee and a plate of pancakes with maple syrup on her bedside table, and carried his own round to his side of the bed. 'You warm enough?' he asked.

'I am. I felt you get up to put the heating on.'

'It's freezing out, looks like snow but it's not. You have anything you want to do today?'

'I fancied maybe going for a drive into Derbyshire, but the roads will be bad there if they're bad here, so maybe we hunker down and just stay warm. We don't know if we'll be needed because didn't they say they would be doing searches and suchlike today?'

'They are, but nobody's here yet. Just the two lads who had the bad luck to pull last night's shift.'

'Should we maybe go to see Lucie's mum? Do you think she'd appreciate or need us there?'

Steve froze. He wasn't ready to face the problems that were certainly heading his way. He sipped at his coffee to avoid answering for a moment.

'I know it's my duty, but Mrs Barker hasn't been interviewed by the police yet, so I think we'd better wait a couple of days before contacting her. But I will.'

Jenna gave a thoughtful nod, and picked up her coffee. 'I can't imagine how she's feeling. The poor woman. And you're right, I didn't think about her having to be interviewed. We'll maybe just stay in and have a quiet day. You think?'

'I think.' He smiled. 'And until the heating warms up the entire house, I don't want to move. These pancakes are delicious – sometimes you Americans have good ideas!'

Steve showered and wandered downstairs a little after nine o'clock, now feeling considerably warmer. Jenna had closed her eyes, so he left her to waken naturally, switched on the kettle and made himself a cup of tea before heading into his office.

He checked through his emails, cleared all of them into the deleted folder, and clicked on Google. He put in LucieB, and waited for the craft shop to appear on his screen.

There was a picture of Lucie, a happy smile on her face as she held up a set of watercolours in one hand, and a bunch of six-inch pads of crafting paper in the other. He stared at her for a moment, remembering the silky feel of her hair when he had placed his hand on her head. A warm head.

He scrolled through her website, noting that it was professional-looking, nothing like the amateur one he had attempted to create giving details of church services and contact numbers.

Different pages had been created for different crafts, and her smiling face appeared on every page showing an example of the one featured as a headline. Her love of crafting shone out of her and he wished he had known her. He also wished he had known of her.

The bang at the door was unexpected and made him jump. He quickly saved the link, and headed towards the front door before the knock had chance to be repeated, ultimately waking up Jenna.

'Adam! I didn't expect to see you. You said...'

'Don't believe everything a policeman says,' Adam France said with a grin. 'You're up then?'

'Well I would have been anyway with that noise. You've certainly perfected the policeman's knock. You need me?'

'Not really.' He followed Steve down the hallway and into the kitchen. 'Just thought I'd check in, because I know I said I was leaving this until we had some results to work with, but the forensic people are all in and I'm SIO, so Elise has bundled the kids into the car and headed off to her mother's house for a few hours.' He took a breath after the long-winded explanation. 'And anyway, I can't get it off my mind.'

'Tea? Coffee?' Steve asked, waving the kettle around.

'Tea, please. I've already had two coffees. I'll be screaming at everybody by lunchtime if I have any more.'

Steve smiled. 'Good choice. I was wired last night after lots of coffee – we had some special stuff bought for us as a Christmas present, and it's truly delicious but very strong. I'm sticking to tea for today.'

'Father Christmas comes to vicars as well then?'

'Certainly does. We had loads of lovely gifts from our parishioners, and lots of them are handmade items they've put a lot of work and thought into. And Jenna bought me a Fitbit. Not sure what she's trying to say, but she wants to make a daily note of my steps! Is she trying to insinuate that I need to lose weight, you reckon?'

Adam laughed. 'Exactly the same thing happened to me last Christmas, and yes, my lovely wife told me exactly why she had bought me one. It must have worked because over the last year I've lost about twenty pounds. Don't knock it, it does make you walk more than you normally would, which can't be a bad thing.'

Steve filled the teapot with the boiled water and gave it a stir.

'Sit down. You want anything to eat? Full English, pancakes, turkey sandwich?'

Adam couldn't help but laugh. 'I have a packed lunch of turkey sandwiches. And I bet Debs has brought the same. She's come in as well, but she's gone round to the graveyard. And no, a drink will be fine. I had some toast with the last coffee. Have you given any more thought to the death?'

Steve sighed and poured out their drinks. 'Thoughts and prayers, as you would expect. Is the post-mortem tomorrow?'

'It was, but like the rest of us, Dr Kirkham couldn't get it off his mind, so he started it at eight this morning. Preliminary results are that Lucie Barker was stabbed twice in the neck, severing the carotid artery, slashing her vocal cords, which would have been the moment when the scream you heard was disconnected. She bled out, and bled out very fast. She then fell head first onto the gravestone, which caused further damage, but Stewart is ninety per cent certain the results will show her death was caused by exsanguination, not the head injury.'

'A minute earlier and I could possibly have prevented it.' Steve looked ill. His face was now devoid of all colour, and he picked up his cup of tea with trembling hands. 'That makes me feel... shitty.'

'Steve,' Adam said quietly, 'you couldn't possibly have affected the outcome. You would have needed advance knowledge, been at the side of the gravestone, and watched every movement the killer made to have influenced this outcome. You didn't even know the direction of the sounds, because by your own admission you wandered around the graveyard looking all over the place. The sound was over very quickly. If you hadn't done what you did, she would have lain there all night until somebody arrived for the Christmas Day service, so don't feel sorry that you didn't save her, feel glad that you found her that night.'

Steve was struggling to collect his thoughts and he sipped at his tea, hoping it would calm his troubled mind. 'So what's next? Checking for a discarded weapon?'

Adam nodded. 'It is. We're not starting that until the tented area has been thoroughly searched and officially noted as cleared, then we'll have the tent removed, freeing up every inch of the graveyard. We have quite a contingent of officers coming over to help us when we're given the all clear.'

'If you need me, just shout up, although I've never done anything like it before so it could be a disaster.' Steve tried to force a smile, but he was still upset by their discussion.

'Thank you, but I'm hoping we'll have enough uniforms. There was no shortage of volunteers after the news leaked that she was so young.' He put down his now empty cup and stood. 'Thanks for the hot drink, it'll fortify me for a bit out there. When my fingers start to drop off, I may pop back for another one if that's okay?'

'Of course it is, and if anybody else wants one, they'll be very welcome.' He escorted Adam to the front door, who turned as he was leaving.

'You know I'll keep you informed?'

Steve nodded. 'I'll be very grateful. This has hit both of us very hard. It's certainly a Christmas we'll never forget.'

He waited until Adam, with a wave of his hand, disappeared from sight, before closing the front door. Stabbed. It hadn't come as a surprise; there had been so much blood visible even without moving Lucie's body – too much blood for it to have been as a result of her head hitting the gravestone.

Jenna was halfway down the stairs as he walked down the hall.

'I heard voices,' she said.

'Just Adam France, we had a chat.'

'They're working?'

He nodded. 'They are. It seems nobody thought it was right to leave it another day. The post-mortem has started and initial reports are that she was stabbed in the neck, but nothing is definite yet. They're starting the fingertip search as soon as the tent has been cleared for removal.'

'Oh, Steve, this is so bad. Can we do anything?'

He shook his head. 'I did say shout up if you can use me, but I got the impression there's a certain amount of training required to do this depth of search, so Adam thanked me and said they had a lot of uniforms coming to help once they were given the all clear from forensics.'

'It's painful to think about it. At any point in my life I would have been on the phone discussing this awful situation with my mum and dad, but I don't want to talk about this with anybody except you. It feels a very personal death. Am I being weird?'

He put his finger under her chin and lifted her face. Then he kissed her. 'You've never been weird, lovely lady. And we can talk it through whenever you feel the need. You want a drink or are you going back to bed?'

'I'm going to jump in the shower, dress in a comfortable

41

jogging suit and chill for the rest of the day. Turkey sandwiches for lunch.' She looked in amazement as her husband sat on the bottom stair convulsed with laughter. 'What did I say?'

'Half the world is having turkey sandwiches today. I've spoken to four people and we've all talked about turkey sandwiches. Oh and apparently that's what DS Jessop has brought for her lunch as well, although I've not spoken to her. We British are nothing if not predictable.'

She climbed around him, heading back upstairs for her shower. 'Put the coffee machine on, vassal. I may require waiting on hand and foot today.'

He stood. 'Your wish is my command, your ladyship.'

She held up a finger in response and giggled as she reached the top of the stairs. Even in such adverse and horrible circumstances, this man of hers could make her smile, make the day seem a little brighter and a little warmer. And he was excellent at getting the correct amount of coffee into their machine...

CHAPTER SEVEN

Adam and Debra stood together and watched as the tent was taken down, packed away and transported to the van.

'We don't know anything,' Adam said, a frown on his forehead. 'This young woman came to a church service and was killed. Why? And on Christmas Day to make things worse.'

'And she's so young. She could have potentially had another sixty or so years in front of her – time to marry, have kids, build her business. It's heartbreaking. I can't imagine how her parents are feeling.'

'We have to talk to them both, see if we can dig a little deeper, there has to be a reason for such a senseless act. We'll wait until we have a bit more information from Stewart, then we'll go see the mother. She can hopefully give us information on Lucie's father, although we need that pretty quickly before any of this hits the news. He's going to be pretty pissed off if he finds out via a newspaper his daughter's been murdered.'

'I'll go and sit in the car, warm myself up for five minutes so I'm not dithering when I speak to her, and give Mrs Barker a ring. I'll ask her for as many details as she can give us even if she doesn't know his exact whereabouts. A full name would be helpful. I suppose it all depends how acrimonious the split was as to whether she knows where he is, but even if she only knows the city, it's a start.'

Adam gave a brief nod. 'Thanks, Debs. You can tell her we'll be round later to speak to her properly, but it will depend on what time we get information from forensics.'

Debra headed down the slope, and Adam walked around some of the grave stones, treading carefully to avoid any icy patches. He headed towards one of the forensic people, who spoke before Adam could say anything.

'Nothing to report, boss. The murder weapon wasn't discovered, so it might be an idea to have wheelie bins in the locality checked. Everything in this churchyard has been lifted, walked around, prodded and poked. It's good that the poor woman was found quickly, we had a head start on looking for anything that could give some sort of hint as to who did this, and we did get blood samples from where she fell, but I suspect it will prove to all belong to her.'

Adam nodded. 'I thought that might be the case. He or she wouldn't discard the knife here, that would be crazy. And I suspect they were in no rush, so could hide it in their coat or bag. I think they probably thought everyone had gone home after Midnight Mass. They didn't know our vicar was still here, and thank goodness he took the time to find the source of the noise that he heard.'

He waited until the graveyard was clear of all personnel, then removed the crime scene tape. It was time to give the church building and grounds back to their custodian, Reverend Steve Rainforth.

Steve handed a cup of coffee to Adam. 'You know nothing further?'

'Not yet. We didn't find anything at all in the churchyard that's of any help, and I know they say every perpetrator leaves something of themselves at the crime scene, but it's not always true. This one doesn't appear to have even been there beyond leaving a deceased young woman.'

'You think it was just a random attack? Maybe they heard me rattling the padlock to check it was secure, because I always do that. Perhaps the intention wasn't to kill, maybe it was to sexually assault her but it all went wrong.'

'It's possible – anything's possible with this one – we have no clue as yet to what happened. I'm going round to speak with the mother after I've finished this coffee, take a statement, see if she's thought of any reason for the attack. But mainly we need to know where Lucie's father is, because unless Angela Barker has contacted him, he won't know his daughter is dead. We need to rectify that before he finds out some other way.'

'So I'm okay to go back into church now?'

'You are. I know you didn't know Lucie as a regular attendee at your services, but was there anybody else in that congregation who was also a stranger to you?'

'Give me a minute while I think.'

Adam waited patiently.

Finally Steve nodded, almost to himself as if clarifying his thoughts. 'I believe there were six. There was a young couple with a baby in a sling, seemed a very young child, there was a lady, an older lady, hair up in a bun, huge scarf around her neck, there was a youngish man, maybe early twenties, and he seemed to be accompanying someone older, possibly his father because there was a resemblance. I believe I knew everyone else.'

Adam swiftly made notes. 'We'll ask for these people to

contact us, just to rule them out. How many would you say in total?'

Again Steve thought carefully, wanting to be as precise as possible. 'I would say maybe forty. I can try, with Jenna and Marjorie's help, to make a list for you, but how accurate it will be is anybody's guess.'

'Marjorie?'

'Our organist, but she's been here much longer than we have, knows everyone. I'll give her a ring, hopefully I can pop round and see her later and we can come up with as comprehensive a list as we can.'

Adam grinned. He liked this man. 'We can't pay you for doing our job, you know.'

Steve hesitated. 'It's personal, isn't it.'

'Personal?'

'My church. I found her, I blessed her earlier in the evening. Yes, it's personal.'

Adam took his cup over to the sink and placed it in the bowl. 'Let me know when you've sorted a list, and I'll pop back to collect it. Maybe we'll have tracked down her father by then, that really is a priority.'

Angela opened the door and stepped aside silently, allowing Adam to enter. He followed her through to the kitchen and she waved at the kitchen table.

'Coffee? Tea?'

He shook his head. 'No, I'm good thanks. I've just had a coffee at the vicarage. We've released the church and the grounds back to Reverend Rainforth.'

'You found nothing?' Her tone was flat, dull.

'We didn't. I'm hoping you can give us some information

about Lucie's father, because we need to ensure he knows about his daughter's death.'

'I'm not in contact with him. The last I heard is he was living in a terraced house that he's bought in Chesterfield. I really don't care whether he knows or not.'

'It was a bad break-up?'

'As bad as it gets. I won't be contacting him, and I don't want him at Lucie's funeral.' She choked as she said the last words. 'I can't believe this has happened. I haven't slept...'

He didn't need to be told. She looked haggard, her hair was screwed up into a ponytail that clearly hadn't seen a brush that day. Red eyes showed the number of tears that had fallen from them, and he suspected she was existing on cups of coffee.

'When did you last eat?' Adam asked gently.

'Eat? Food?' She frowned. 'I have no idea.'

'You have bread?' He walked towards a roll-top bin on the side, clearly marked BREAD. He removed two slices, popped them into the toaster and went to the fridge. Angela simply stared at him.

He removed the margarine from the fridge, and took a small plate from a cupboard. Three minutes later he placed two slices of toast in front of the distraught woman and said, 'Eat.'

Despite his earlier words, he made them both a cup of tea, and slowly she began to recover. Very slowly.

A little colour returned to her cheeks, but there was still no hint of a lessening of the angst and turmoil inside her. 'Thank you for this,' she muttered. 'And you're here to tell me nothing?'

'We still don't have the full post-mortem report and it would be wrong of me to speculate. I believe Lucie didn't suffer, didn't know it was happening...'

'I'm suffering.'

'I know. And I wish I could tell you something that would

comfort you a little, but we are right at the beginning of the investigation, hampered by losing yesterday to Christmas, but everyone is in today and working. It's affected all of us, especially the ones who were first on scene. To feel so helpless...'

'I'm sorry,' Angela said quietly, stifling a sob. 'I'm being a cow. I'm just thinking about myself, it never occurred to me how it would affect everybody else. It's so hard, she's my only child.'

'It will be a couple of days at least before we can begin to trace your ex-husband – the council, unlike the police, don't work over Christmas – so if you have any information at all, make of car, phone number, that can help, we need it. We have to try to reach him before this becomes public knowledge, and I think we may only have hours.'

'I can tell you the car he was driving when I threw him out. I can even show you a picture, but I'm not saying he's still got it.'

'It doesn't matter, DVLA will have an address on record for the car. You said his name's Philip Barker?'

'It is. Middle name bastard. Give me a second to get the picture up on my phone.'

She removed the iPhone from her pocket and began to scroll. It took a couple of minutes, and then she showed him a picture of Philip and Lucie standing either side of a BMW. He could see the registration clearly.

'Can you send it to my phone, please?'

Seconds later he was forwarding it to Debra, asking her to chase it up. If Barker still had the car, they could access it and have an address within minutes.

'I have to go, you may have helped more than you know,' he said. 'I promise when I know anything about Lucie I'll be back. You promise me you won't hide away, that won't help anyone, least of all Lucie.'

She nodded and walked to the door.

Angela watched as Adam drove away. 'You know nothing,' she said quietly. 'Nothing.'

CHAPTER EIGHT

Philip Barker was easily traced. He still had the same car, and the vehicle was parked outside his home when Adam and Debra arrived to give him the sad news of his daughter's death.

They had to knock three times before he opened the door, his hair standing on end, his eyes bleary.

'What?' he demanded. 'Who the fuck are you? Don't you know it's Christmas? I don't want any of whatever you're selling...' He stared at the warrant cards held out by both officers.

'Can we come in?'

He held the door open a little wider. 'If you must.'

They followed him down a hallway that didn't look in any way festive, or clean. The carpet felt sticky as they walked, and the kitchen held no appeal whatsoever. Dishes were everywhere, evidence of a Christmas meal having been cooked and eaten, but not cleaned and tidied away.

'What do you want?' It left his mouth almost as a growl.

'We're here to inform you of a death, sir.' Debra was determined to be polite.

'I hope it's my ex-wife,' he said, smiling for the first time.

'No,' Debra said sharply, 'it's your daughter, Lucie Barker.'

He sat down with a thud on the kitchen chair. He ran a hand through the hair that was still like a halo around his head, as if suddenly realising this was no joke. The words had been serious.

'Lucie? What's happened?'

'She died in the early hours of Christmas Day, under suspicious circumstances.' Adam stared at the man who was visibly crumpling in front of him. 'I can't give further details yet as we don't have a complete post-mortem report, but it is definitely not a death from natural causes.'

Debra moved to the sink and picked up a glass, she rinsed it out several times, and filled it with water.

'Here, have a drink, you look as though you could use it.'

He nodded his thanks and drank half the contents. 'Thank you,' he said. 'I needed that. Is there nothing more you can tell me? You don't know who did it? And how has Ange taken it?'

'Your ex-wife is obviously distraught,' Debra said, 'but like you, still knows nothing of what has happened. We were keen to reach you as it's going to be in the news shortly, and Lucie is your daughter even if you're no longer with your wife.'

'She's not, strictly speaking. Ange was three months pregnant when we got married, so technically I'm her stepfather. But she's always been my daughter, we gave her my surname and brought her up as our child. I never knew who the genetic father was; I did ask, but Ange always said it was a one-night stand and she couldn't remember his name.'

Debra and Adam exchanged a quick glance. It was looking as though you had to ask the right question if you wanted an answer from Angela Barker.

'That was a brave thing to do,' Debra said, 'taking on another man's child.'

'It wasn't brave at all,' he said. 'I loved her as my own, but I've lost both Ange and Lucie now anyway. Alcohol and stupidity go hand in hand in my life.'

They waited but he didn't expand on the statement.

'So what now?' Barker asked.

'Where were you just after midnight as Christmas Eve became Christmas Day?'

'I was here, pissed as a newt as the saying goes. I went to the pub until about eleven – the one just round the corner, the Brown Bear – then realised I was struggling to see and walk, so I came home, laid on the sofa and woke up about eleven on Christmas morning. Christmas used to be good, it isn't now. I've nobody to alibi me after eleven on Christmas Eve, I'm sorry.' He dropped his head onto his arms that were resting on the table, and his shoulders heaved. 'Dead,' he said. 'Lucie, dead.'

'We're going to need a statement, Mr Barker. Debra will take it and get you to sign it. I'm just going round to the pub to get your alibi covered for Christmas Eve and then we can leave you alone.'

Adam walked into the pub, and was engulfed by people. It was busy and he approached the bar hoping to spot whoever the landlord might be, but in the end he asked a female member of staff who was clearing glasses off tables.

'That'll be me,' she said, looking him up and down. 'Who's asking?'

Adam showed his warrant card and she waited, offering no further words until she knew why he was there.

'I won't keep you,' he said. 'Do you know Philip Barker?'

She smiled. 'Everybody knows Phil. He's a regular.'

'Was he in Christmas Eve?'

'He was. He only lives around the corner, and he was

absolutely steaming drunk by about half ten. He gave in at eleven and went home, but I followed him until I saw him go through his front door. I wasn't sure he'd make it all the way without landing in the gutter. Then I came back here to the rest of the merry crowd. Didn't see him Christmas night though, figured he was still recovering.'

'Well he looks rough today.' Adam smiled. 'I'm guessing from the state of his kitchen and the number of empty bottles and cans, he had some alcohol in for the Christmas season. Thank you for your help, you've confirmed what he told us. I won't tell him you followed him home.'

Debra craned her neck to see out of the passenger window as they drove back from Chesterfield to Sheffield. 'I've been past that spire so many times,' she said, 'but I can't help but be mesmerised by it whenever I see it. I'm sure it's got a proper name, or the church will have anyway, but everyone still calls it the Twisted Spire.'

'Maybe the architect designed it after he'd been in the Brown Bear all night. It's certainly a popular pub; it was heaving when I went in. And it's a landlady, not a landlord. I got the evil eye when I asked for the landlord. Barker signed his statement?'

'Very shaky signature, as you can imagine, but yes, he signed it. He asked me what he should do, and I couldn't tell him anything. I'm pretty sure Angela Barker doesn't want to know him, but neither of them has given any reason for the break-up. Wonder if it was down to his drinking. He does seem to take it to excess, he looked shocking.'

'Well, I feel pretty safe in saying he couldn't have got from Chesterfield to Sheffield on Christmas Eve in the state he was in. The landlady confirmed he was legless – she actually followed him home to make sure he got there without being killed. And he couldn't have driven without killing somebody else, so we need to look elsewhere.'

Debra nodded. 'I agree. I also got the impression that he loved Lucie, loved her as his daughter, not a stepdaughter. I think he was waiting for us to go so that he could have a damn good cry.'

'I'm sure you're right. Can you just text the team and tell anyone who's at the station that we're having a briefing in about half an hour, please?'

'We've got nothing to brief on.'

'I know. I'll blag my way through it, hope that something comes in from forensics. We can at least report that we found the father, so that's a weight off my mind.' He indicated to turn into the car park, and pulled in behind a squad car.

'Let's grab coffees and head upstairs. Hopefully we'll have some of the team in. I want to check my emails before we start the briefing, could do with seeing something inspirational.'

The emails weren't particularly inspirational, but there was a detailed post-mortem report. He made relevant notes then headed towards the briefing room where six people were in attendance. He began by thanking everyone who had forfeited Christmas, then moved on to the report.

'It appears that Lucie Barker did die from exsanguination, caused by a knife wound to the neck. It severed her vocal cords and sliced through the jugular, so she would have bled out very quickly. The head wound was caused by her fall onto the headstone of the grave and did not contribute to her death. Lucie was only twenty-four years old with everything ahead of her. We have to catch whoever did this and get them locked up.'

Adam paused for a moment as he glanced through his notes. 'Debra and I visited a man called Philip Barker, who was Lucie's stepfather, but married her mother before Lucie was born, so is in effect, her father. He's no longer part of the family, but was visibly upset when we delivered the news to him. He lives in Chesterfield, and we have ruled him out of being in Sheffield on Christmas Eve – he was too drunk to stand up.'

'Have we ruled anybody in?' PC Vicky Leeson spoke from the back of the room.

'Not yet. The whole world seems to be in a fug of alcohol, wrapping paper and twinkling lights. Tomorrow's Friday, so I'm hoping things start to wind down until we get to next Tuesday evening and we have fireworks and stuff to contend with.' He glanced around. 'Any questions?'

'Does Lucie Barker have siblings?' The question came from a serious-faced DC Ivor Newman, and Adam shook his head.

'No, she didn't. It makes it so much worse really, knowing she was an only child. Her mother is distraught, looked awful when we called round. She's clearly at odds with her ex-husband though, but no details on that as yet.'

'We doing a room search at Lucie's home address?' DC Kenny Patrick asked. 'Hilary and I can do it, if that's what you need.'

'Thanks, Kenny. And don't ring first, just turn up, be polite and make it clear it's not an optional thing, you're there to do your job.'

Kenny nodded and glanced across at DC Hilary Crane. 'We'll go first thing tomorrow?'

'Fine,' she said. 'You driving? Do I need extra life insurance?'

Adam grinned. 'You drive, Hilary, then we might get you both back in one piece. I know I don't really need to tell you, but keep your eyes peeled for a diary or a journal, let's see if we can find out a bit more about the late Miss Barker. I'm sure there's something we've not discovered yet, and I'm hoping she's left some clues somewhere. We're also going to have to search her shop premises, because there may be something there that would point us in a different direction.'

Adam paused to organise his thoughts into something that made sense. 'At the moment we only know her family, but surely she must have had some other side to her life. Hilary, ask Angela Barker for her daughter's shop keys when you go, please. They're not in her bag that we recovered from the crime scene, so they must be at home. Or in her car, which I'm guessing is still at home. She apparently walked to the church on Christmas Eve.'

'Yes, boss,' Hilary said. 'We'll go through the car carefully in case it needs to be forensically examined at some point. Gloved and booted. We might just find something.'

Adam nodded his thanks and looked around at everyone. 'Do we all have jobs for tomorrow?'

There were nods all round. 'Okay, now go home. Let's salvage a little bit of Christmas and make a start in the morning. Report back as soon as you have anything to pass on to the rest of the team, and we'll have an afternoon briefing tomorrow. Now go home,' he ordered.

CHAPTER NINE

Adam drove into work with a smile on his face as he thought about the previous evening. Santa Claus had delivered a family gift from Adam's Aunt Margaret who lived in Kent, and it had proved to be the hit of Christmas as far as all of them were concerned. She had sent an upmarket bingo game, complete with a drum that automatically delivered the balls, and the entire evening had been spent with William and Alfie taking it in turns to be the caller.

It turned out that the boys played bingo at school as part of their maths lessons, and they certainly had the patter off to a fine art. *Two little ducks, twenty-two, have you got it – probably not*, had been the mantra for every number called out, and Adam guessed it was the way the numbers were called at school.

There had been much hilarity, and Adam had actually won a Mars bar for getting a full house. This explained the smile on his face as he parked his car at the police station, and he knew he would remember the phrase 'probably not' for ever.

It was quiet in the briefing room but the peace didn't last long. It seemed nobody wanted to stay home and keep the magic of Christmas alive – that had disappeared with the finding of Lucie Barker's body.

Friday began with a general discussion, and everybody agreed there was a complete lack of viable suspects, and in fact they were doing very well at ruling people out.

'Why did her parents separate, boss?' Hilary Crane asked. 'Was it something to do with Lucie?'

'I don't know.' Adam frowned. 'Both of them spoke of the split, but the way it was mentioned, it was just a parting of the ways. I got the impression from Philip Barker that his overuse of alcohol was a contributory factor. If we ever need to bring either of them in for a deeper interview, that question will have to be answered, but I let it go in view of the fact that they might be living apart now, but they are grieving parents. If there is any hint that lies have been told, or omissions made that could be relevant, one or both of them will find themselves answering us officially in an interview room.'

'Thanks for clarifying that, boss. I was reading through all the reports and I just felt that tingle you get sometimes. There's a reason why a twenty-four-year-old is still living at home with Mum when she had a place of her own to move into at one point. She was quite an independent young woman, a business of her own, and suddenly she cancels her new home, stays with Mum. And he leaves. Is there more to that situation?' Hilary leaned back with a sigh. 'Just my thoughts,' she said.

'Excellent thoughts,' Adam responded. 'And I do believe at some point we'll have answers to all the points you've raised, either accidentally in conversation or by getting them officially. However, Philip Barker does have a pretty solid alibi for Christmas Eve – he was simply too drunk to walk properly, and unbeknownst to him he was actually followed home from the pub and the landlady watched him enter his house. And let's not forget he lives in Chesterfield. It's quite a trek to Sheffield when you're drunk out of your skull. No, it wasn't Philip Barker, and instinct says it wasn't Angela Barker, but as always, open minds are our greatest tools.' He looked around the room and grinned at everyone. 'And here endeth the first lesson. I guess I've seen too much of our Reverend Rainforth.'

'Well don't ruin everything by suggesting him as a suspect,' Debra said with a laugh. 'I've fair taken to our local vicar.'

'So far there's nobody else left to suspect,' Adam retaliated. 'We need everybody to return to work, for life to get back to normal, and we need Lucie's bedroom and business to be searched. Hopefully something will stand out as being not quite normal, and we can take it from there. I'm really struggling to believe this was just some random attacker out on Christmas Eve looking for somebody to kill. Lucie Barker was targeted for a reason, and somewhere in her life is the answer. Could a woman have done it? Without a doubt. There was only one slash with the knife, straight across her throat. It wouldn't take strength, just a desire to kill. I'm saying that because we can't write anybody off because of their gender.'

People began to disappear to work on the various jobs allocated to them, and Adam and Debra finished off their reports of the previous day while waiting for the keys to arrive that would give them access to Lucie Barker's craft shop.

With the keys finally in their possession, and apparently after objections from Angela Barker who didn't want them to be in the shop without her supervision, Adam and Debra opened up the door and entered the alarm code.

They stood for a moment taking in the splendour of LucieB's, and Debra exhaled. 'Wow,' she said. 'This is a crafter's dream. My dream, anyway. And I have absolutely no idea where we start to look through everything. It's awful to think she had built it up to this level of excellence because she had a passion for crafting, and now she's gone.'

Adam thought for a moment. 'Presumably it will all pass to her mother, to Angela Barker...'

Debra stared at him, following his thought pattern. 'No, surely not. She wouldn't kill her own daughter just for financial gain.'

Adam shrugged. 'Worse things than that have happened during my career. She had no alibi, she simply confirmed she walked to the church looking for Lucie because she didn't like the idea of Lucie being alone on the walk home after the service. It was only when she saw the forensic van that she headed back. She didn't go and ask somebody what was going on, she explained it away as burying her head in the sand, not really wanting to think her daughter could be late home for a reason, and that reason had drawn the police to the churchyard. It's all very sketchy and flimsy on her part, but I occasionally have to remind myself that life can be like that. Not always cut and dried.'

'So you thought you'd just wind me up about the possibility of Angela being involved in the murder, just for the fun of it?'

'No, just trying to ram home the stuff I was saying at the briefing about keeping a fully open mind. Of course I don't give serious credence to Angela having killed Lucie, but we've been a bit quick dismissing that thought. Let's start upstairs, get as much done as we can, and see if anything arises.'

The stairs to the upper floor began at the opposite side of the shop to the main door, and Debra switched on the lights as she reached the top. It was just as wonderful upstairs as it was downstairs. There was a tiny office area in one corner, and Debra headed towards that. It contained a small two-drawer filing cabinet and she began with the bottom drawer. It held an accounts book with absolutely nothing written in it, so Debra guessed Lucie was using an online system for her accounting. She had a folder for invoices that had been paid, and a wages book that was up to date for two employees. Their salaries were definitely on the miniscule side so she had to assume that they didn't work many hours, just helped out maybe when Lucie had a class to teach, or when she needed to buy new supplies. It wouldn't be practical to keep closing the shop; she would have needed assistance of some sort. She took a photograph of the two names and addresses, and moved on to the top drawer.

This contained a couple of reams of printer paper, printer inks, business cards and other bits and bobs of stationery – nothing that said 'look at me, this is a clue to why I was killed'.

She did a thorough check of the rest of the small space but didn't find anything that was in any way helpful. She looked at Adam and shook her head to indicate there was nothing, and went out to join him as he searched the rest of the upper floor.

'Anything?' he asked.

'I've two names and addresses we can check on, but they seem to indicate part-time workers, and not on a regular basis. We need to check them out, but I can't see them being of any help. We maybe need to speak with her accountant, because I think she possibly uses an online accounting system – no handwritten book-keeping anywhere. Her mother may know more about that. You found anything?'

'No. This is a proper Aladdin's cave of stuff I know nothing about. Who knew diamond painting was a thing?'

'I did,' she said, trying not to laugh.

'Well I do now too. Not sure I want to have a go, but I'm expanding my brain cells to take all of this in, encompassing every craft under the sun.' He waved an arm around, indicating the wealth of kits bought in by a smart shop owner.

'Let's have a mooch around downstairs and see if anything leaps out at us, but this all looks fine so far,' Debra said.

Adam nodded, his mind blown by the multitude of stuff he'd already looked at.

The downstairs area held a whole wall of knitting wools, and Adam chose not to comment. His mind was reeling – he could never have imagined anything like this, and he kept thinking about Lucie Barker, who had clearly put her heart and soul into making a success of her business, and was now lying in a mortuary.

They finished their searches and checked all lights were off and the alarm reset before closing the automatically locking door behind them.

'Seeing something like that makes everything so much sadder, doesn't it?' Debra said as Adam switched on the ignition. He pulled away from the shop before answering her.

'We've got some real villains on our manor, some of them I honestly don't give two hoots about whether they live or die, but this case has knocked me for six, especially now that I've seen what this young woman had achieved. She definitely didn't deserve what happened to her and we need to make sure we bloody well find out who took that knife to her, and why.'

'You still don't think it's just a random act, then?'

'No, Debs, I don't. It feels targeted, but it seems nobody knew her, never mind enough to target her. We've a lot more digging to do before we get the answers we need. And we need to start at the beginning. I don't buy this one-night stand lark, I believe Angela knows who the real father of Lucie is, and I suspect Philip Barker believes that as well, and it's played on his mind enough to force a rift in their relationship.' He took a deep breath, jumped on his brakes as he noticed the traffic lights turning to red, and swivelled slightly to face his sergeant. 'But will she tell us the truth?'

'She might, now there's nobody to hide it from. You think she might talk to me, woman to woman, rather than you? Happy to try if you think it'll do any good.' Debra laughed. 'Nobody to hide it from except the real dad, I mean?'

CHAPTER TEN

S teve Rainforth couldn't settle. He'd lived a sheltered life,
had rarely come into direct contact with any sort of
crime, so to be plunged headlong into a murder where
he had been the one to find the victim was mind-blowing.

Spending Friday afternoon putting together a sermon for
Sunday morning that could touch on the events of Christmas
Eve without involving the word nativity was proving difficult.
He currently had a bin half full with scraps of paper on which
he had jotted down thoughts knowing they were rubbish and
didn't merit being transferred to his computer.

He read through the small amount he had felt was maybe
satisfactory, and shook his head. Utter rubbish, he decided. He
closed his laptop, stood and walked over to the window. To his
surprise, snowflakes were drifting down. There was the
lightest of covering on the ground but he felt heartened by it.
Snow was his favourite weather, and he stood for some time
taking in the beauty of the flakes. Hearing Jenna's voice
calling from downstairs to tell him it was snowing made him
smile.

He headed down, went to stand at the back door to revel in

the reality rather than staring through a window, until Jenna pointed out it was turning a bit chilly with the door wide open.

'Sorry,' he said, closing and locking the door. 'I'm just a big kid when it comes to snow.'

'Pork and turkey curry for tea tonight. It will help us keep warm now we appear to be embroiled in arctic conditions.'

Steve laughed and pulled her into his arms. 'Hardly arctic conditions, I doubt there's a quarter of an inch of the white stuff, but the curry will be very welcome. Is that the last of our Christmas meat?'

'Sort of. I've cut all of it up, and the rest is in the freezer. So it'll turn up intermittently, disguised as curries, or pies, or even the odd sandwich. You married a thrifty wife, I'm afraid.'

He kissed her cheek. 'I married the right wife.'

She nodded in agreement. 'You definitely did. Sometimes I get things wrong, but mostly I'm perfect.'

He left her to do a quick stir of the slow cooker contents, and walked through into the lounge where he asked Alexa to play Gold radio. They were both fans of music from the sixties and seventies, and it always amazed him when he heard Jenna singing along, knowing all the words to the songs.

He felt a little lost. He had no doubt that the information given so hurriedly by Angela Barker concerning the parentage of her daughter was accurate – the age of Lucie tied in with the time he and Ange had been so in love. And he was certain she hadn't known of her pregnancy when she had told him she wanted out of the relationship because she could never match his aspirations of a life in the church.

He had immediately applied for training and within a week was at college, at peace with his God, not so much with his heart. And he never heard from her again. A friend told him some time later that she was married and had a baby, but it never occurred to him for a minute that the baby could have been fathered by him. And now it seemed that was truly the case.

He needed time with Ange, time when they could freely discuss what had happened, and why he hadn't been allowed to acknowledge his child. His only child, pending whatever was to come over the next few months.

Was it possible Lucie had hung around outside the church waiting to speak to him on his own? Now he felt even more guilty. Maybe he was inadvertently the cause of her death. If it wasn't for him spending a few last minutes having his Christmas conversation with God, she wouldn't have been waiting amongst the gravestones, possibly trying to hide from concerned members of the congregation who would have queried if she was okay. Those few minutes of delay gave someone time to cut her throat, and he would never be able to forgive himself for that. But could he confess that to Ange?

Adam was also enjoying watching the snowflakes that drifted by his office window, not convinced it would settle and would probably all have disappeared by the time he left to go home.

He was frustrated by the lack of information and had an uncomfortable feeling he needed to get deeper into the relationship that had fallen apart, the marriage of Philip and Angela Barker. He felt as if the whole issue had been dismissed, especially by Angela, and he had to let her know that wasn't going to continue. He would have her collected and brought into the station where she would be formally interviewed. If that still didn't give him the answers, he'd bring Philip in as well. One way or another he would have the reason behind their break-up, and how it had affected the late Lucie Barker.

For the first time in almost ten years, he could have devoured a cigarette. He used to do his best thinking with a cigarette in his hand and a packet in his jacket pocket. On the day Elise had giggled her way through telling him she was pregnant, he'd decided he couldn't be both a smoker and a daddy, so he stopped. And now, watching the lazily drifting snowflakes, he wanted a cigarette.

He sighed, returned to his desk and took out a packet of Trebor Extra Strong mints. They could be a substitute in the absence of any tobacco.

Debra was still working at her desk, and he sent her a text telling her to go home. He watched her read it, hold up a thumb without even turning round to look at him, and carried on staring at her computer screen.

He was closing down his own computer when Debs appeared in his doorway. 'Why did the Barkers split up?' she asked.

He grinned at her. 'Hopefully we'll find out tomorrow, I'm bringing Angela in for interview. Wouldn't be necessary if I hadn't felt she was hiding something, but I'm sure she is. I'm not saying it's definitely relevant to the case, but we'll decide that, not her.'

'You need me in?'

'You got something planned?'

'Depends whether this snow sticks or disappears.'

'Okay, don't come in. For Christ's sake, we've basically worked all Christmas, so no, I don't want you in tomorrow. See you Monday, enjoy the weekend.'

Debs nodded. 'Thank you. I've hardly had chance to open my presents yet.'

Five minutes later he was watching her make her way very carefully across the car park. The snow wasn't melting, and the

ANITA WALLER

flakes falling from the heavens were definitely bigger than they had been half an hour earlier.

'Go home, Adam,' he said to himself. He gave a brief nod as if agreeing with his own thoughts, and sat back down at his desk. He opened up his computer again and reread the reports posted by the various members of his team. Nothing stood out that made him stop and think, except there was nothing to stand out. One dead young woman, and nobody could come up with any idea why it had happened.

Why was she still in that graveyard? According to Steve Rainforth, he found her some twenty-five minutes or so after the end of the service. Why was she still hanging around on such a bitterly cold night? And who the hell had been watching her? The post-mortem results showed no evidence of sexual assault, so what had this young woman done, or what did she know, that merited her being killed so brutally? And if the vicar hadn't taken his time coming out of the church, she might have lain on that gravestone until the following day.

He sucked in his breath. Could she have been waiting to speak to Steve? Could Steve have possibly said something in his sermon that touched her, that she perhaps felt she needed to query with him?

He rang Steve's mobile number, and it was answered within seconds.

'Adam?'

'Hi, Steve. Just a query that I thought you might be able to help with. Do you keep your sermons?'

'Funny question,' Steve said with a laugh. 'But yes, I do. I have to be careful not to repeat myself, so I save every document. You want the Christmas one, don't you?'

'I do, although it's a stab in the dark. I can't for the life of me work out why Lucie Barker was still in the churchyard, and it crossed my mind she maybe wanted to speak to you, possibly about something in the sermon.'

'I'll email it. Tell me your address.'

Steve repeated it back after writing it down, and they said goodbye.

The email arrived within a minute, and Adam opened the attachment. 24 Dec 2024 was the file name and he leaned forward to read it on his screen. It wasn't of any great length, but it was well-written and quite... poignant, was Adam's thought as he read through to the end. It spoke of the birth of a baby, one that was loved at the moment of birth by its parents, but ultimately became loved by an entire world, in varying degrees. And it didn't matter which religion a person followed, they still knew of Jesus.

The last part was the bit that made Adam take stock. It was so true, and yet he had never thought of it in such simple terms.

He read through it a second time, and couldn't for the life of him imagine which part of the sermon Lucie could have possibly wanted to discuss with a vicar she didn't know, at a church she hadn't visited before.

And why was she there alone? Had she insisted on going on her own? Adam had got the impression that Lucie and Angela were close, close enough to share a home, close enough for Angela to have invested initially in Lucie's business, close enough for Lucie's death to have caused devastation to her mother.

He read it a third time and realised he was actually enjoying the words, the flow of Steve's thoughts, his utter belief in everything he said. He sent it to the printer – he wanted Elise to read it, he knew she would see what he was seeing, somebody who believed in his God, and who knew how to express that belief.

As he walked across to collect the printout he glanced

through the window. The snow was starting to become a bit ominous, so he folded the paper, slipped it into his briefcase and zipped up his coat.

It looked like he was going to have a potentially long drive home, with the possibility of having to use the shovel in the boot to dig himself out of trouble. If indeed the shovel was still in the car... Hadn't they needed it to bury the cat after her demise earlier in the year? He groaned. Why was his life never straightforward?

He put his briefcase in the boot, saw the lack of any digging implements, and cursed under his breath. He rang Elise, said to expect him when she saw him, and to say goodnight to the boys for him because it could be a long journey home.

'Okay, Sherpa Tensing,' she said. 'Take care. Oh, your shovel's in the garage, so don't go looking for it.'

He got in the car, stared at the ignition key in a threatening manner, daring it not to start. To his utter relief it did.

He reversed out of his space, drove to the gates, and looked with a degree of horror at the completely ungritted road. This could be a long night.

CHAPTER ELEVEN

A dam cancelled work on Saturday and Sunday. His plans to bring Angela in for questioning and possibly Philip Barker as well were postponed.

The Frances loved where they lived on the edge of the Derbyshire village of Hathersage, just not when it snowed during the working week. Adam had no choice but to stay home, so the weekend was spent using different modes of transport for the entire family, the four sledges that lived in the garage, alongside Adam's snow shovel.

He forwarded the email of the sermon to Debra for her to read in case he had missed something obvious, and she responded by saying she couldn't see anything to query, certainly not at just after midnight on the start of Christmas Day. She did add that the words were beautifully written, clearly from the heart, and not just in note form. Steve had written his sermon exactly as he had wanted it to come across to his congregation. She did add a comment that maybe they were barking up the wrong tree and it wasn't Steve she was waiting to see, but somebody unconnected with the church. Another question to put to Angela when they eventually managed to interview her.

He felt strangely pleased that both she and Elise had responded exactly as he had responded to Steve's words, and he almost wished he had been at the service. He didn't doubt he would be at the 2025 Midnight Mass...

The snow stopped falling by lunchtime on Saturday, and gritter lorries began to appear – very slowly. He didn't fancy walking from Hathersage on Monday morning, and wondered briefly if he could talk somebody in a squad car into coming out and getting him, but then decided that was cowardice of the highest order. All he had to do was remember to put his shovel in the boot and all would be well.

Adam was in work by seven on Monday morning, a bit achy after a weekend of snowball fights, sledging, and digging out their home. He was halfway to work when he thought about the shovel still in his garage, and had to hope that Sheffield City Council had worked hard on their roads over the weekend so he wouldn't have to go back to collect it.

It was a reasonably clear journey, and he pulled into the station car park with a sigh of relief. Debra was already there, as were Hilary and Ivor, but nobody was in the briefing room.

He guessed their thoughts had taken them straight to the canteen for bacon butties and coffees, so his own boots mirrored their footsteps. His entire team were in and seated around one table. He took some ribbing for being the last one to arrive, but eventually they conceded that okay, they didn't live in Derbyshire, so he had a valid excuse.

To punish them he said he would have paid for breakfast, but as they were already sorted, he'd just get his own...

By eight o'clock DC Kenny Patrick and PC Vicky Leeson were pulling up outside the home of Angela Barker. Vicky felt a little nervous, she wasn't normally chosen to take part in such activities as bringing someone in for questioning. Her skills were computer based, and she usually found herself sitting at her desk providing information for everybody else to act upon.

Kenny turned to ask if she was okay. She nodded and opened her door. 'Let's get this done, get her back to the station. I feel bad enough having to bring her in, she's just lost her daughter.'

'Will you still feel bad if she's the one who's killed her?'

Vicky's mouth opened, then closed without saying anything. There wasn't much she could say.

Kenny knocked on the door, and it seemed to take for ever before it was opened.

Angela stared at them. 'You have news?'

'No, Mrs Barker. We need you to get dressed and come with us to the station.' He pushed on the door, and Angela allowed it to open. The two officers stepped inside, and she turned to head down the hall, clearly still sleepy and not understanding what was happening.

'Go with you? Why?'

'I understand DI France has some questions, and we need to take your statement anyway. PC Leeson will accompany you upstairs and wait for you to get dressed.'

'Can I get a drink? I took a couple of sleeping pills last night and my mouth is so dry I can hardly swallow.'

'Vicky, can you get Mrs Barker a glass of water, please? And then we really do need you to get dressed, Mrs Barker.'

Angela's temper was beginning to surface by the time they reached the station.

Her bag and its contents were taken from her at the desk, and she was led to an interview room to wait for the arrival of DI France.

Adam took his time. He wanted answers but he wanted them to be accurate. She would be at the cocky-as-hell stage at the moment, but in half an hour she would have progressed to the nervous stage and be more inclined to speak to him truthfully. All he wanted was to find out what she was hiding, because he sensed she knew something that hadn't surfaced yet.

He stood with Debra looking through the observation-room window at their guest. 'She looks awful,' Debra said. 'You seriously think she had something to do with this?'

'No, but I think there's something she's not saying. I'm hoping it's nothing major, and we can run her home again very shortly. I really don't want her to have played any part in what happened to Lucie, but unless she opens up about the daily life of her family, we won't be able to exclude her. And we need her to formally identify Lucie now that can go ahead, so I need to organise it with her. Maybe she'll feel able to do it today.'

They stood for a further five minutes, then moved to enter the room.

'DI France and DS Jessop entering the room. Present is Angela Barker.'

Angela stared at them both. 'Do I need a solicitor?'

'Anytime you feel you want one, we can stop this interview and get a duty solicitor for you. Generally it takes a couple of hours, but we can do it,' Adam said with a smile. He read her rights to her, and she looked completely blank.

'Are you charging me with something?'

'No, definitely not,' Debra said. 'We have to read you your rights to protect both you and us. If anything you say does end up being repeated in court, it will be admissible. It wouldn't if we hadn't explained your rights to you. Does that make it clearer?'

Angela frowned, then nodded. 'I suppose so.'

'Good. And if you have further questions, just ask us.' Debra smiled at the woman in front of her, who was now starting to look more uncomfortable than angry.

Adam opened up his file as he began to speak. 'Thank you for coming in, Angela.'

'Did I have a choice?'

'No, not really, but I understood you to have been compliant, didn't cause any problems for our two officers. Believe me, not everyone is like that.'

'When can I see my daughter?'

Adam produced a piece of paper. 'I have the pathologist's release form here, and a request for official identification to take place. When we've finished, I can have you taken to see her, or we can do it tomorrow.'

'No, please take me today. I need to be with her, even if it's only through a window.'

'We can arrange for you to be in the room with her, if that's what you would like?'

She nodded, wiping away her tears. 'I would.'

'Okay, let's get on with it then. Can you tell me about Christmas Eve? Start at around seven o'clock and tell us how the evening transpired.'

'Around seven?' She closed her eyes for a moment. 'We'd finished eating, and we'd cleared the dishes away. We sat down to watch television, although don't ask me what was on because I was reading. It was just background noise as far as I was concerned. We had a hot chocolate and Baileys around nine, and it was while we were drinking it that Lucie announced she thought she would go to Midnight Mass. I was a little shocked, but she said she'd been considering going to church for some time, and what better time to start than Christmas Eve. I said she couldn't drive there, and I couldn't take her, because we have a zero alcohol and driving rule in our house. She said she would walk, it's not much more than half a mile.'

'You didn't want to go with her?'

'No. As you saw when you turned up, I knew the vicar several years ago and I didn't want to put him in a difficult position by seeing me again. We were a couple, but I gave him up because his calling was clearly to the church and I really had no time for it. I couldn't bear the thought of being tied to religion. I saw his name in a local free paper and it said which church he was at. We couldn't have lived any closer. And that was the church Lucie chose to attend for her first Midnight Mass.'

'What time did she set off?' Adam's eyes were locked onto Angela's face. He felt she was telling the truth. But was it the whole truth?

'About half past ten. She went far too early, but she said she would prefer to get there before everyone else, hang around the churchyard until people started to arrive, then go in with them. I made her wrap up warmly, it was such a cold, frosty night. It didn't save her though, did it?'

'We've had her phone checked, and it seems the last call she made was to your number, at one minute past eleven.'

'That's right. I asked her to let me know she'd got there okay. She sang to me.'

'Sang to you?' Debra looked surprised.

'She has... had a lovely voice. She sang "Silent Night". Twice actually. First in English, then in German. She loved the German version best. I said something along the lines of *you're a silly bugger, Lucie Barker*, and we laughed before saying we loved each other. That's the last time I spoke to her.'

Adam glanced at his notes. 'You said you began to feel uneasy about one o'clock?'

'That's right. I expected her home before that, so I walked towards the church, fully expecting to meet her on the way. It was still bitterly cold and I was rushing to try to warm myself up. I got almost to the churchyard when I saw the police cars and vans.'

'You didn't ask what was happening?'

'No. It's like... not wanting to believe what you're seeing. I convinced myself she must have taken a different route home, even though there isn't one. I didn't go to bed, I waited. And when you turned up, I wasn't surprised. The only thing that did surprise me was seeing Steve Rainforth again after all these years. He looked a little older, but I knew who he was, without any doubt. And you brought me the worst news possible. It was definitely a silent night for my Lucie from that moment on.'

CHAPTER TWELVE

Adam leaned back and stared at the distraught woman sitting across from him. He felt shitty making her go through the whole thing again, and in much greater detail. Her feelings were showing, unlike any interaction they had shared before.

'Let's take a break,' he said quietly. 'Hot drink, Angela?'

'Tea, please,' she said, grabbing another tissue.

Debra stood. 'DS Jessop leaving the room.'

He waited until Debra had closed the door before telling Angela to relax. 'We're not here to lock you up for life,' he said with a smile. 'We're here to find out what happened to Lucie, and why. So don't say anything until we restart the recorder, enjoy this drink because I imagine it's your first of the day. Am I right?'

She nodded. 'You are. I was woken at eight by two thugs, who actually proved to be okay. They allowed me a drink of water, and at least I could swap my pyjamas for jeans and a jumper, but it was a hell of shock. It's put me off being a criminal, I can tell you.'

'Score one to us then,' Adam said with a laugh. 'We were very impressed with Lucie's shop when we went to look at it.'

'Such talent,' Angela said. 'She could do anything. Sang like an angel, could make anything she set her mind to making, she was an amazing person.' She sighed. 'And all those gifts she was blessed with are gone now. It's so hard to accept, and I keep finding myself talking to her, even though she's no longer here.'

The door opened and Debra re-entered with a large teapot, three mugs and milk and sugar balanced somewhat precariously on a tray. 'We need to leave it a couple of minutes, then I'll pour. Everything all right?' She waited a moment before telling the recorder she had re-entered the room.

Both Adam and Angela nodded, indicating they were okay and hadn't come to blows in her absence. 'We've talked about Lucie,' Adam said. 'A very talented lady.'

'I guessed that when I saw her shop. Will you keep it going, Angela?'

'I don't know. I don't have the skills my daughter had, but I can do certain stuff. I'm the tutor for the wool side of things. I teach crochet and knitting, with all their variations, and Lucie concentrated on everything else. There are a couple of ladies who help out when needed, and I spoke to both of them last night to tell them the shop would be closed until I could get my head around everything. They said not to worry about them and they would return if and when I decide to reopen, but I don't know what to do.'

'You'll know when the time is right,' Debra said gently. She gave the tea a quick stir, then poured out their drinks and handed them around. 'Angela, you said Lucie didn't have a boyfriend?'

'No, not for some time. She concentrated on the shop, said men would only distract her. Why?'

'Just making sure we haven't missed anyone out who could

be a potential suspect. We have a long list of people to interview who were all at that church service. Reverend and Mrs Rainforth put their heads together and came up with a comprehensive list of everyone they could remember. There were only three who they didn't know or haven't been able to work out who they are.'

'I can't stop thinking that if I hadn't been stupid about seeing Steve again after all these years, I would have been at that service with her, and none of this would have happened. I would have kept her safe, we would have walked home together.'

'Or you both would have died that night,' Adam said gently. This distraught woman was clearly blaming herself for not looking after her daughter as well as she thought she should have.

'She wasn't a child, your Lucie. You can't blame any of this on yourself, Angela,' Debra said. 'Lucie was twenty-four, making her own way in the world and absolutely making her own decisions. Which she did by walking to that Mass on Christmas Eve.' She sipped at her tea. 'What we really need to know is why she didn't immediately set off for home, but remained in that churchyard for a small amount of time. Long enough for someone to attack her. Think back to when she said she wanted to go to the service. Did she perhaps suggest she might meet up with someone?'

Angela shook her head. 'No. I would have told you something as big as that by now, trust me.'

Adam nodded, then clicked his biro as he pulled a notebook towards him. 'So now we have to dig a little deeper into the depths of your family. You said Lucie was moving into her own place, then Philip and you decided to split up, so she put the move on hold and stayed with you.'

'That's right. She knew I was struggling with the massive

change in Philip, his excessive drinking that was happening every day, and the rapid decline in our savings because he was taking out so much money. It was constant.' She breathed deeply, then sighed before continuing.

'We had a huge argument one day, and he promised to get help. He went to one AA meeting, decided it wasn't for him, and never went back. Then one night everything seemed to explode, and he was gone by the morning. I haven't seen him since, and as far as I'm aware, neither had Lucie. I think she would have told me if she had, even if it was only accidental. The divorce was handled by solicitors so we didn't have to speak. Lucie and I settled down to a quiet life, no more fear, no more worrying about a swift punch to the head, or him grabbing an arm and twisting it up my back, a bite somewhere where it wouldn't be seen...'

Debra winced. 'What caused the explosion?' she asked.

Angela looked down at her hands, and the two officers could tell she was starting to clam up. Had he attacked her so badly she had feared for her life? She had been fairly open about a relationship that had soured, mainly through alcoholism.

'Angela,' Debra repeated. 'What caused the explosion? Did you involve the police?'

She gave a dry sort of laugh. 'No, no police. That would have been the end of me, and possibly Lucie as well.' She froze as she seemed to realise what she had just said. *Possibly Lucie as well.* 'No,' she breathed the word. 'No, he wouldn't kill his own daughter.'

'He has an alibi,' Adam said. 'He was in the pub, and it was some considerable distance from here, in Chesterfield. He went home around eleven, and I know he could have got here by midnight, but he was almost paralytically drunk. So drunk that the landlady followed him home to make sure he got there and didn't just lie down in a garden and pass out. She confirmed he was staggering around, barely able to walk, and we saw him the next day. He was ill, believe me. He isn't under any suspicion of killing Lucie.'

Angela visibly relaxed. 'I know it sounds strange but that's such a relief. It seems he hasn't changed one bit. Once an alcoholic always an alcoholic in his case. He always enjoyed a pint, but until… oh, maybe five years ago… it was once a week we would go out, and it was kind of like our date night. We had a good life. Then suddenly he started calling at the pub on his way home from work, then drinking in his lunch hour, with the eventual cancellations of work at his factory, and it suddenly got to the point where he seemed to be permanently drunk, permanently vicious and scary. I'm dreading him attending the funeral because I know he'll be drunk before he gets there, and he'll cause trouble.'

'Don't forget we'll be there,' Adam said. 'If he's too bad, we'll chuck him in a cell overnight to sober up. That tends to work as a temporary fix. So tell us what happened on that last night.'

Adam could sense Angela was holding something back, knew it was possibly massive in her mind, but not really relevant to solving who killed her daughter. They just needed the complete picture, and the only person who could fill them in was Angela.

She shook her head. 'Please don't make me go through it. Isn't it sufficient that you know he was made to leave our home?'

'No, it's not. This is why we had you brought here today, not because you're a suspect, but because it's very obvious you're withholding information, and that in itself is a criminal offence if it proves to be relevant to the case.'

She sipped at the dregs of her tea and placed the cup gently on the table. She lifted her eyes to stare at the two officers. 'Okay. Lucie had gone to bed, the atmosphere in the house was awful. She waved her Kindle at me, said she was going to read herself to sleep and she'd see me in the morning. Philip had arrived home from the local pub roaring drunk, so I made myself a Horlicks to take to bed with me, fully expecting him to crash on the sofa for the night. I left the drink in the kitchen, went round making sure all the doors were locked, then went back to the kitchen to collect my drink. Philip was there, holding a strip of tablets that I assumed were paracetamol, because he waved it at me and simply said "headache".'

She paused for a moment and the two officers waited. They didn't need to speak, Angela was getting there, delivering yet another puzzle piece they hoped would help solve who killed Lucie Barker. And why.

'I picked up my Horlicks, gave it a final stir, and went to bed. I read, sipped at the drink, but the next day when I cleared it away there was still half a cup remaining. Fortunately. I dread to think how things might have turned out if I'd drunk the whole cupful before falling asleep.'

Adam smiled in encouragement. 'The tablets? Not paracetamol?'

She shook her head. 'No, some sleeping tablets my doctor once prescribed for me, but because I felt scared by how deep a sleep they made me have and how rough I felt the next day, I stuck them in a drawer never to be used again except in cases of extreme emergency. I believe he'd added four tablets to the drink.'

They waited. Was this showing Philip Barker in a more murderous light? Had he wanted to get rid of his wife? Her death from an overdose of strong sleeping tablets could be construed as suicide...

Angela leaned back. She stared at the two people forcing her to relive one of the most horrific experiences of her life, and one she didn't want to repeat to anyone, especially police officers. 'I was sound asleep when I heard screams. I thought it was in my dream. I sat up, I was alone. The screams were heartbreaking and I got out of bed, but struggled to walk. By this time, I'd told myself the screams were from outside and I managed to get to the window to look out into the back garden but then I realised the awful sound was in my home. And it was Lucie screaming. For a few brief seconds, and in my befuddled state, I thought Philip was dead and Lucie had found him.' She paused for a moment. 'If only that had been the case...'

They waited, not wanting to interrupt the flow of her words.

'I staggered to Lucie's room, the screams were awful. I pushed open her door and Philip was on top of her. He was raping her.'

CHAPTER THIRTEEN

Tears were rolling down Angela's face. Adam felt like the worst bastard under the sun, and Debra stood, moved around the table and hugged the distraught woman.

'I'm so sorry,' she whispered. 'So sorry we had to make you do this, but we have to know all the facts if we're to move forward.'

Angela was struggling to speak, although it was more like she was struggling to breathe. 'I live with this every day,' she gasped. 'Every time I open Lucie's bedroom door I see his naked body forcing himself inside my daughter. As you know,' she sobbed, taking big gulps, 'she's only a slip of a girl, and she simply couldn't move him. When we spoke afterwards she told me she didn't even know he was in the room until he was on top of her. She had been fast asleep. Maybe he drugged her in the cup of tea she took upstairs with her, we'll never know, but his actions certainly woke her up.'

She grabbed another tissue. 'I'm so sorry. You'd think with the passage of time it would get easier, but it doesn't. I've not laid eyes on him since, I dragged him off her, kicked him in the balls and pushed him downstairs. He was roaring drunk as always, and that maybe saved his sorry life, because he kind of stumbled to the bottom, but my own strength felt superhuman. He must have left his clothes in the lounge because I heard him unlocking the door so I went to the window to see what he was doing. He was fully clothed as he left the house. I stood at the window for a short time watching for his next move, I didn't want him coming back inside. He was clutching his balls so I'm guessing he was in some pain, but he managed to stand in the middle of the road screaming obscenities. I never told Lucie what he said.'

'Which was?' Adam asked gently.

'She's not my daughter so I can fuck her.' Angela choked once again on her sobs.

The two officers glanced at each other. This hadn't been what they expected her to say, none of it. The rape victim was now dead, leaving the only two people who could speak of it to be Angela and Philip Barker. CPS would refuse them permission to take it any further. Angela would say she saw him raping her daughter, he would say it didn't happen, she must have been hallucinating after taking too many sleeping tablets.

'Who is Lucie's father?' Debra said quietly, hoping to coax the truth out of her.

'I don't know. I went to a party, had too much to drink and woke up in a strange bed with a strange man by my side. I can't say I felt as though I had been raped, but three months later I had to confess all to my parents. By this time I had met Philip, and I told him I had to stop our relationship because I was pregnant. At that stage we hadn't done anything more than kiss and hold hands, and he said he wanted to marry me. He would bring the baby up as his own, and nobody need ever know she wasn't his.'

'So Philip at this point in his life wasn't an alcoholic?'

'Definitely not. And up to about five or six years ago he wasn't, but he changed, became depressed, and he turned to drink. Since then he's lost his company because he's never fully sober and hardly ever went to work. Now I don't care whether he's drunk or not drunk, he means nothing to me. What the rape did to my daughter mentally was the worst part.'

'Because she saw him as her dad whether he was drunk or sober?'

'That's right. And he must have been so rough with her, really forcing himself inside her, because there was considerable bleeding. I tried to get her to go to the doctors, but she refused. Said she just wanted to forget it all. But it changed her. She had been making plans to convert the attic area of the shop into a home. It's currently empty, she doesn't use it for storage or anything,' she hesitated, 'didn't use it, I mean. I'm sorry, I keep forgetting...'

'Would you like to go and see Lucie now?' Adam felt he was walking on egg shells; she suddenly seemed so fragile. 'Then Debra will take you home. We'll have your statement typed up while you're with Lucie and get it sent down for you to sign before you go home. Thank you for your openness, Angela.'

She stared at him. 'You're going to bring Philip in, aren't you?'

'Too damn right we are. Would he drink and drive?'

She laughed. 'Without even thinking about it. But you said he had an alibi for Christmas Eve.'

'He has an alibi up to the point where the landlady of the Brown Bear watched him go into his house at about half past eleven, but if his neighbours speak of his car moving after that time we need to know about it. If nobody saw him leave his house, or his car move, that's fine. Could he murder Lucie?'

She shrugged. 'Who knows. I would never have thought the lovely man I married would ever drink to the extent that he does, so I guess I'm not the right person to ask about him. And he was a good father up until that point.'

They logged off the recorder, and Debra took Angela's arm. 'Come on, we'll go and have a cuppa in the canteen, I'll pre-warn them we're going to do the formal identification of Lucie, and then I'll take you there.'

'And I'll see to this statement,' Adam said. 'You have our numbers if you think of anything else. Take care, Angela.'

Angela stared through the viewing window at her daughter's body. 'Yes,' she said quietly, simply letting the tears flow unchecked down her face. 'Yes, that's Lucie Barker, my daughter.' She pressed her hand on the glass, as if by doing this she could touch Lucie.

Debra waited patiently, knowing the grieving mother would eventually turn away of her own accord. And she did.

'I will see Lucie, touch her, when she's at the funeral director's place. I simply can't do it today. You'll let me know when I can arrange her funeral?'

'Of course. Let's go into this office, I need you to read through your statement, then sign it once you're happy. You need to confirm we got everything you said down correctly. I'll run you home after that. Would you like a cup of tea? Coffee?'

Angela shook her head. 'No, I'm good, thanks. Let's get this signed and I can go home and crawl into bed. I can't remember the last time I had a decent sleep.'

Debra took out the statement from the file on the desk and passed it across to Angela. 'Take a few minutes to read through it, then sign it.' She handed her a pen and sat back to wait.

Angela read everything twice, occasionally sighing, then with a flourish she signed her name. 'Can we add to this that if you find out who did this to my Lucie, that you have to give me the name first?'

Debra shook her head. 'Sorry, no. I'm sure if we did that, there would be no need for a trial. Then we'd have to lock you up.'

'I'm serious, you know. I could quite happily kill whoever has done this, because they've blown apart my life. And it's so irritating that I'll probably be the last one to be told. Whoever has done it will be locked away long before I'm told their identity.'

'That's the way democracy works, I'm afraid. I don't always agree with it,' Debra admitted, 'but we have to do what's right.'

'And what will you do about Philip? I've given you information that he's a rapist. What happens now?'

The Crime Prosecution Service won't touch it. Because the victim has died, it's your word against his. The CPS won't waste public money going for a prosecution unless there's a damn good win in it for them.'

Angela nodded. 'I guessed that would be the case. I wanted Lucie to report it on the night it happened, but she kept saying he was her dad and she wasn't going to report him. I was still befuddled by the tablets I didn't know I'd taken, so didn't push it, but I wish I had.'

Debra stood. 'Come on, let's go and have a cuppa at yours and talk about Lucie. They'll manage without me for the afternoon.'

Adam could feel serious anger building in him. He had quite liked Philip Barker; he had clearly had a hangover but had still come across as a pleasant chap despite the fact he would never in a million years pass a breathalyser test.

He had no reason at all to doubt what Angela Barker had

disclosed. It had been a reluctant divulging of information that they had pushed her to give, and now he wanted to hear what Barker had to say about it. Would he admit to it? It wouldn't take a genius to work out that he wouldn't be charged for it, so he would have nothing to lose. But did that give him a reason to kill his daughter? With her dead, life would be considerably easier for him. The threat would magically disappear. But did he have reason to think she would go to the police? The marriage was well and truly over, he must have felt pretty secure that the rape would never surface.

He glanced at his watch. Just after three. He walked out into the briefing room to see who was in, and asked DC Kenny Patrick and DC Ivor Newman to commandeer a squad car and go pick up Barker.

'Don't mention what it's in connection with, just tell him we need a formal interview and a signed statement. If he's not at home, try the Brown Bear just round the corner. And go in and get him out if he's in there.'

The two officers gave him thumbs up, understanding exactly what he wanted. A bit of intimidation always worked wonders at loosening tongues.

They knocked twice before deciding Philip Barker wasn't home. 'He's either doing odd jobs for the neighbours who need a little help in their lives, or he's in the pub,' Ivor said, peering through a window. 'It certainly looks deserted inside.'

'Helping neighbours? I got the impression from the boss that was something this feller definitely wouldn't be doing. Come on, let's head to the pub.'

They could have walked, but decided it would have more of an impact if they parked the squad car in the pub car park. 'Best lock the doors,' Kenny said with a laugh, 'the car might have gone by the time we come out if we don't.'

They walked slowly across the car park, aware that the vehicle would already have been seen. They had a choice of rooms, but guessed their target would be in the bar, not the lounge.

Kenny went to the bar, and the landlady moved towards him. 'Officer?' she said.

'We're looking for Philip Barker.'

She looked around. 'He's still not here. That's more than strange. He's always in on a Monday because he makes up a foursome for dominoes. Those three chaps on that table in the window might be able to help, they're his domino cronies. You've been to his house?'

'We have. No answer.'

'Was his car outside? He parks it on the front garden.'

'Yes, it was.' The two officers looked at each other.

'We'll go back and knock again. Thanks for your help.'

They drove back to Barker's house, and knocked twice. 'I'll go and look round the back,' Ivor said.

Kenny waited, then the front door opened. It wasn't Philip Barker who stood there, but Ivor. 'The back door was unlocked. I'm going to check upstairs.'

Kenny nodded, and began to look around the ground floor.

'Shit!' Ivor's expletive made Kenny's heart sink. He headed for the stairs.

'He's dead. There's tablets and booze everywhere.'

'Ambulance?'

'It's too late for that. I'll ring the station.'

Kenny went into the bedroom, the smell making him gag. Philip Barker was half hanging out of the bed, and life was definitely extinct.

CHAPTER FOURTEEN

It fell to Adam to pass on the news of Angela's late husband's demise, and he saw tears spring instantly to her eyes.

'I know it's stupid to react like this,' she tried to explain, 'but until he started to drink heavily we had a pretty good life, full of love, no financial problems, and I thought we'd always be together, supporting our daughter as she started her adult life. I miss those times, and I'm sorry he's dead. It all could have been so different if only he'd not given in to the drink.'

'Forensics are there at the moment because although we believe it to be suicide, we have to be sure in view of the situation with Lucie. He did leave a note of sorts. It's just a scrap of paper, but as soon as I saw the words I remembered what you said he had shouted. The note said *She's not my daughter*.' Adam watched for her reaction to that detail.

'But she was. Oh, not genetically, but he was her dad in every way. And I can only assume he's guessing I would tell you about that awful night. He couldn't face the consequences of what he did, could he? Maybe he thought you could bring charges.'

'We'll never know. I'm just sorry I had to bring you this news so soon after losing Lucie.'

She stared at Adam. 'Please tell me I won't have to be the one who identifies him for you.'

He didn't answer, simply looked at her.

'No,' she breathed. 'You can't ask me to do that.'

'You know it only takes a second, just to look through a window and say yes it's him.'

'And then I can forget he was ever in our lives?'

'If that's how you see your way forward, yes you can.'

She briefly closed her eyes. 'When do you want me to go?'

'I'll let you know. We can take you, and it will possibly be Wednesday.'

'I'll go on my own now I know where it is. It's funny, you go through life never even knowing where the mortuary is, and now here I am, visiting it twice in a few days.'

'Thank you,' Adam said. 'I'll contact you when I know we're clear for viewing.'

'Did he suffer?'

'Pills and alcohol in huge amounts. He meant to do it, but he wouldn't have felt pain. And I believe it would have happened fairly fast, although I'm no expert in things medical.'

'Thank you for telling me, but I can't grieve for him. My thoughts are all with Lucie, and I don't want any details of his funeral or Coroners' Court, because I won't be attending either. Is that understood?'

He nodded. 'It is. I'll leave you to do whatever I've stopped you doing, and I'll ring when we know you can identify him.'

She watched as Adam pulled away, and leaned her head against the windowpane. How could anybody's life implode in such a spectacular fashion, and so quickly? If someone had said on

Christmas Eve that she would feel like this a few days later, totally bereft and not knowing what to do next, she would have laughed at them, would have said of course I'm not going to feel like that. But she did.

And now she had to go for a second visit to the mortuary to identify the rapist. That DI knew he was asking too much of her, yet he didn't withdraw his request, just patiently waited until she agreed to do what he wanted.

Manipulated, that was the right word for how she felt. It had been a long time since she'd actually seen Philip. Would she be able to confirm it was him? Excessive alcohol would have changed his appearance, and going by what DI France had said, his alcohol consumption was off the scale.

She went to make herself a cup of tea, needing something to calm her frazzled nerves and soothe thoughts that had become increasingly tempestuous. She had detested Philip for so long that she had no idea how to handle his death, how to deal with her feelings about losing a man she had lived twenty-two years of her life with.

There had been so much anger, but he had almost destroyed Lucie mentally. Physically she had recovered; he had used so much force he had injured her but time had solved that issue. Time hadn't sorted out her fear. Even on that last night, on Christmas Eve, she had suggested she might slip her keys into her bag, just in case. She had joked about how to hold them in your fingers to make a handy weapon, but then she had decided against it. *I'm off to church,* she had said, *God will keep me safe.*

Angela carried her tea through to the lounge and sat on the sofa, raising the footrest. She hugged the mug and took a sip. It burnt her tongue but she didn't care. At least a burn was a genuine feeling. She had felt cold as ice since the police, and Steve, had arrived at her door on Christmas Day.

Steve. She had fought against loving him but the first time

they made love, both of them virgins, she had fallen completely head over heels for him. She didn't want to love him. She knew where his destiny lay, and it wasn't in the real world; it was in the world of the Church of England.

The look of devastation on his face when she had told him she couldn't see him again, that she needed to put distance between them, had been awful. But she had been right. She wasn't vicar's wife material. But then she realised why she felt sick all the time. It wasn't unhappiness causing it, it was the tiny foetus growing inside her.

By then she had seen Philip a couple of times, but when she tried to call off their budding romance and told him the reason why she had to end it, he put on his knight's suit of shining armour and rescued her. And nobody but the two of them knew that Philip wasn't Lucie's father, not even Lucie, until a few days after she had thrown him out of their lives and their home.

Angela sipped at her tea, wondering how everything had gone so drastically wrong in her life, and why this God that Steve cared so much about could have deserted her in such a spectacular fashion.

She felt her own life was over. Without Lucie it didn't feel possible to live.

Steve stared at the white screen on his computer. He had typed Sunday 5 January 2025 and been instantly distracted – that date would have been his mother's seventieth birthday if she had lived, the woman who had championed his wish to become a vicar.

He missed her, and allowed himself a few minutes to simply sit and think about her and his father, both together again. They had been loving parents, supported him through everything, been so proud of him, and in thinking of them his thoughts once again turned to Lucie.

He didn't doubt Angela had told him the truth as she was in the early hours of knowing she had just lost her daughter; the grief had erupted out of the woman he had once loved. The dates fitted, Lucie was definitely his daughter, and he felt saddened knowing he would never have been allowed to be part of her life because of the actions taken by Angela all those years ago.

The brief phone call from DI France to tell him of Philip Barker's death had rattled him. His thoughts once again drifted towards contacting Angela, but in the early stages of an investigation he guessed he would definitely be out of line. Maybe a phone call…

He returned to planning the sermon with a sigh. He always added a touch of his personal life, even if the congregation didn't always realise it, but adding any part of his current life definitely wasn't going to happen.

Maybe he should talk about the three kings? A comparison with royalty in the present day. He had a lot of time for King Charles, and the Norwegian king was a good bloke. He picked up a pen and began to jot down disjointed thoughts that would, hopefully, transport as proper sentences to his screen. He did rather want to get Christmas well and truly out of the way; it certainly wouldn't stand out as one of their better festive periods.

There was a small tap on his door and he looked up to see Jenna waving a mug of tea at him. 'You want?' she said.

'I definitely want,' he answered, smiling at her. 'Come and write a sermon for me while I drink it.'

'You're stuck?'

'Distracted more like. I typed in the date for Sunday, and it's Mum's birthday. She would have been seventy. She was a lovely mum, and while she's always in the corners of my mind, birthdays and suchlike hit me like a ton of bricks. So that took my thoughts away from what I was supposed to be doing. I'm hovering around the three kings, comparing them with present day kings, but I'm not convinced they won't all fall asleep while I'm talking.'

'Does anybody ever fall asleep during your sermons?'

'I have no idea, but it's why I always have a rousing hymn straight after I've finished speaking. That wakes them up if they've nodded off.'

She laughed. 'I'll leave you to get on with it. Enjoy your tea. I'm going to turn up the heating, grab my Kindle and have a quiet day. I'm feeling out of sorts, so I might ring Mum later, check they're all okay.'

He sipped at his tea. 'Give them my love, and tell them we'll definitely be out for a visit this summer.' He smiled at her. 'If all goes well with this IVF stuff, we may have news for them.'

'That would be wonderful,' she conceded, 'but I don't think anything will happen quite that fast. But one day we'll have our baby, I'm sure of it.'

She closed the door behind her after blowing him a kiss, and he returned to his computer with a sigh. 'Alexa, who is King of Norway?'

On hearing that it was King Harald the fifth, he made a swift note on his pad. Maybe it was worth a go at weaving some magic into three present day kings. He had another chat with Alexa and discovered Felipe the sixth had been King of Spain since 2014, so he added him to his list. He now had his three present day kings. Time for a bit of research, and a bit more from his cup of tea. Then he smiled. Stephen King. He dismissed that thought as quickly as it had drifted into his mind.

Gold, frankincense and myrrh – which present-day king would have delivered which gift? He smiled to himself at the strange way his mind was working. Christmas hadn't been good this year, and maybe he could get some humour into what he was writing, lighten the mood a little within his congregation. Because by the time he delivered this sermon, most of them would have had a visit by the police, as Lucie's killer was still an unknown quantity.

CHAPTER FIFTEEN

Tuesday the 31st December, New Year's Eve, the biggest party night of the year, and the snow had almost gone.

The briefing room was full at eight o'clock that cold morning, and most of its inhabitants were drinking coffee to wake them up fully. The meeting the day before had told them schedules were being prepared for visits to the congregation who had been in church on Christmas Eve, and they would be expected to clear their lists in one day.

This crime needed to be solved. It felt as if it was at a standstill, caused by Christmas itself and the death of the victim's father. 'We have to push on with this now. Christmas officially finishes after tomorrow so by Thursday I want solid results, everyone who's on this comprehensive list of attendees at that Midnight Mass should have been interviewed, and we're putting out an appeal for the possible three people we haven't been able to give a name to as Reverend Rainforth said they were newcomers. Somebody must have seen something and maybe don't realise they're holding the key to what happened later.'

Adam paused for a moment to switch his mind from Lucie to Philip. 'Philip Barker's body, as you know, was found yesterday. Although we're awaiting final toxicology results, it seems it wasn't a suspicious death. He took a huge overdose of assorted tablets, and a lot of whisky and vodka. However, we think Philip believed a secret was about to come out, and the secret was that he'd brutally raped his daughter, Lucie Barker. Once again drink was an issue, and Lucie's screams brought her mother to her rescue, but by then he had done considerable damage. He left the home that same night, and neither of the two women have seen him since. I know you'll have questions once you start to digest this information, but our concentration has to be on finding Lucie's murderer.'

He glanced around the room, giving his brain time to decide what needed to be said next. 'Vicky, I need every taxi firm in Chesterfield and the surrounding area contacting to see if they picked up Philip Barker on Christmas Eve. If you find a yes to that question, we'll obviously want all the details. I have to say I don't believe Lucie's death had anything to do with Philip, but ruling out a taxi will help. He was actually too drunk to walk, and he wasn't acting. The pub landlady followed him home, unseen, to make sure he didn't fall over in somebody's front garden. She watched him stumble through his own front door before she returned to the Brown Bear.'

Vicky held up a thumb in acknowledgement that she understood his instructions, and then held up the lists she had prepared. 'All the visits are on here, and because it's a local church there's nobody from outside the area. In other words, everyone on the list will live quite close to everybody else on it, and definitely quite close to the church. Thank goodness it wasn't Sheffield Cathedral.' She finished with a smile.

'Thanks, Vicky. And if any of you have any queries while you're out and about, contact Vicky because she knows more than I do. I want detailed reports uploaded before you go home, because while you lot are watching football or partying to see the new year in, I'll be reading your accounts.' Adam's words were said seriously. Vicky did know more than he did. He was starting to feel as if he knew nothing at all. It was now almost a week since Lucie's brutal death, and while he knew about the lifestyle of Angela and Lucie, that was the extent of his knowledge.

And he felt there was a lot more he should know.

He left the briefing room with instructions that everybody should be on their way by nine, and anyone they didn't manage to contact had to be listed for follow-up later. He sat on his chair with a thud, feeling somewhat disgruntled. He now had to wait, to hope that somebody had seen something out of the ordinary, and that just one bright PC from the crews that had gone out to do the interviews would pick up on it.

Jenna was baking a cake, deep in concentration. She flinched as Steve came up behind her and encircled his arms around her waist. 'You made me jump!' she complained, then turned to kiss him.

'Sorry,' he said. 'I'm off out. Mandy Newbould has just rung to say Sarah's slipping away fast, so I'm going round to be with them. I don't know when I'll be back...'

'Don't worry,' Jenna said. 'Just do your job, and send my love to the family. They'll all be in my thoughts and prayers.'

He gave a brief nod, kissed the top of her head and went to get his coat and white collar. He briefly considered taking the car, but decided it wasn't worth the effort. It was only a five-minute walk to Sarah's house, and he could compose his thoughts on the way. He had known the family since day one of his arrival at the church – they had all arrived bearing a bottle of wine, flowers for Jenna, and a welcome card.

He closed the door quietly, slipped through the garden gate linking the vicarage to the churchyard, and stopped at the grave where his daughter – he was still struggling with that knowledge – had died, alone and without any chance of rescue. It seemed her death had been very quick, yet he still thought if only he had found her sooner...

He paused for a minute, said a short prayer for her soul, then brushed away a recalcitrant tear that threatened to roll down his cheek. He headed for the path and then out of the church gate at the bottom.

Five minutes later he was knocking on the door, then being admitted.

Sarah was very close to death. Her breathing was almost non-existent; there were such long periods between breaths. Mandy and her husband, Keith, were sitting side by side, both holding her hands, talking at odd moments to her.

'Steve's here, Mum,' he heard Mandy say, but Sarah was too close to leaving this earth – she wouldn't have a clue whether he was there or not.

Mandy's sister stood and indicated Steve should have her chair, but he shook his head. He moved towards the top of the bed, and placed his hand on Sarah's thin, wispy grey hair. She didn't stir.

'Sarah, may the Lord bless you and keep you as you leave us to be with Him. May He surround you with His angels on your journey, and let you know how much you are loved and always will be here on earth. Your pain and suffering is almost over, Sarah, and the love of everybody in this room goes with you. You can let go now, sweet lady, and finish your journey. I send you on these final steps with the blessings of the Lord God Almighty, Father, Son and Holy Ghost, amen.'

There were whispers of amen, and within three minutes it was over. Her breath had stilled, and tears flowed from everyone. The attending nurse confirmed she had died and sent for a doctor for the officiality required at such a time, but Steve moved out of the room and into the kitchen. He wanted the family to have last precious moments with her.

Keith followed him and shook his hand. 'Thank you,' he said. 'That woman is so loved, and you have helped ease things, believe me. It's like she was waiting for you to arrive.'

'We've been close for a long time now,' Steve said, 'as you know. And really all she wanted, as so many dying people want, is permission to leave this earth. She passed within a few minutes of me saying it was time to go. We now have to learn to live with it, and it's going to be hard for me to announce it in church on Sunday, she's been such a supporter of Jenna and myself ever since we arrived.'

Keith nodded. 'She thought the world of you. You want a cup of tea? I've been sent in here to put the kettle on, because everybody thinks it will solve all problems.'

Steve smiled. 'It usually does. And I will have one, there's absolutely no reason for me to rush back. I'm trying to write a sermon about the three kings and find a new angle on it. But it's because I'm trying to avoid the obvious, the thing I should be talking about, which is death not being final. Your mother-in-law's passing is my third in a week, and because of police activity that will be common knowledge by the end of the day. Not Sarah, but the other two, which are linked.'

'With the awful couple of weeks we've had I've not really followed what happened at the church. They've not said anything about an arrest then?'

'Nothing. I've given them a list of names, everyone who was at the church for Midnight Mass, but to be honest they'd all gone home. The church always empties quickly after the late

Christmas service because people want to get home and go to bed. Christmas Day is hard work for most people. Lucie, the lady who died, was also at the service, but for some reason was still in the churchyard. I don't suppose we'll ever know why.'

'A tragedy,' Keith said as he switched on the kettle. 'Just like that is in there, losing Sarah. She's been my mum rather than mother-in-law for so many years, and I don't know what I'll do without her.'

'She was in pain, Keith. She isn't now.'

Keith nodded. 'I know. I keep telling myself that. It'll be a strange world without her though.'

He got several mugs, and poured milk into a jug. 'You take sugar?'

'No thanks,' Steve responded.

'I'll not get it out then. We've all been trained not to have it,' he said with a smile. 'Even Sarah, who had a proper sweet tooth.'

'I know. Whenever I popped round to see her there was always chocolate biscuits, and she loved a KitKat. She'll always live on in my mind. She was the first to welcome us here, and I don't forget kindness like that. It's hard to believe she's gone.'

The kettle switched itself off and Keith poured water into the biggest teapot Steve had ever seen.

'Has Sarah left any instructions?'

'She has, but Mandy has all that in hand. I'm keeping out of it, find it all too much.'

Keith stirred the pot and poured several cups of tea. He handed one to Steve who sat the kitchen table with it, placed one on the table for himself, then loaded up a tray with the rest. Keith picked it up and then put it back down. 'I've made one for Sarah,' he said quietly, and began to cry.

CHAPTER SIXTEEN

By ten to nine the small fleet of squad cars had all but disappeared from the car park at the station. They had their lists, their questions, their notebooks for recording answers given by the unsuspecting congregation members, and their intuition, always on high alert for this type of job. Sometimes they just knew...

Adam and Debra watched them go. He was deep in thought, considering that life was much more exciting as a DC than it was as a DI.

'Should we go and talk to somebody?' he asked.

'If you want. Who do you want to talk to?'

'Stewart. See if the post-mortem has shown anything other than what we expect it to for Philip Barker.'

She nodded. 'Is it just part of our natural make-up that we don't believe anything we see?'

'It is. There should be an exam for it. I've got a bit of an inkling that Angela Barker isn't exactly lying, she's simply not telling the truth, the whole truth, and nothing but the truth. She's holding something back. Okay, I think it probably is suicide in Philip Barker's case, but did he know for certain we knew about the rape? Did she contact him and tell him she'd told us? In his drunken state he would probably see no way through it...'

'She's a hard nut to crack, boss. Whatever has happened, she's not going to admit it, and I wouldn't mind betting you're right. Come on, let's go see what Stewart has to tell us, but if Philip's completed suicide because she told him we now know about the rape, in my book that's murder. And she's got away with it. The awful thing is, if I was in her shoes would I have acted any differently? Our kids come first, last and middle, we defend them at all costs.'

'And she was certainly very close to Lucie. We'll leave her be for a couple of days then do a revisit. We need to know exactly what she's keeping from us.' He slipped on his jacket. 'Right, let's go find out what we're dealing with re Mr Barker, and then we need to know if he has next of kin we need to notify. He may still have parents who probably know nothing about the way his life has panned out. I would hate them to read it in a newspaper.'

Debra nodded. 'I'll text Angela and ask her. She can't be classed as next of kin, they divorced, and I'm not sure who'll be responsible for his remains.'

Adam laughed. 'She probably won't even respond. Come on, let's stop putting off this morgue visit.'

Stewart was reading through the toxicology report and adding the details to his post-mortem revelations, when Adam and Debra were shown through to his office.

'You haven't brought me another body?'

Adam shook his head. 'Not today. We're here for results, or any you have that can tell us for definite how Philip Barker died.'

'It was undoubtedly self-inflicted. Only the most recent fingerprints on the vodka and whisky bottles, only his fingerprints on the tablet ephemera, the packets and suchlike. Nobody helped him, and he meant it. The alcohol in his body was through the roof and I don't know how his brain hadn't exploded – I've put actual readings in the official report, but take it from me, there was enough alcohol in his system to have killed him without the tablets. I think he'd been drinking all day and all night. It wasn't just spirits, there were empty cans of lager, even an empty sherry bottle. He'd obviously decided to go out with a bang, and it worked.'

'That's so sad,' Debra said. 'So sad that anyone could feel life wasn't worth living, but this man had an illness, alcoholism, and he could have recovered with help.'

Stewart nodded. 'I've had four suicides over the past six weeks or so, and alcohol has been a factor in every one of their deaths. Mr Barker has been the most alcohol saturated one, but it really is a sad state of affairs when you reach a point like that in your life. You know, I can handle accidental deaths, murder, natural end of life deaths but not self-inflicted death. It just seems so... pointless. I think that's the word I need.' He stood. 'Follow me, I've cleaned Mr Barker up as I thought you two might turn up.'

'His ex-wife's coming in, hopefully tomorrow, to formally identify him, so I'm hoping he doesn't look too unlike the man she remembers from a couple of years ago, or whenever was the last time she saw him.'

Stewart led them into his autopsy room, and slid open the fridge door. He unzipped the body bag and both Adam and Debra reluctantly stepped forward. Neither of them relished viewing any deceased person, and they stared down at the face of Philip Barker.

Everything about him was grey. His thinning hair was grey,

his moustache and the stubble around his chin was grey, his skin was grey. Adam looked at Debra, all too aware that she did this part of her job with reluctance. She nodded at him to show she was okay – at least this body, unlike his stepdaughter's remains, didn't have a slash across the throat.

Debra gently laid her hand on the body bag. 'I hope he's at peace now. To drink to excess in the way that he did, he must have had such a miserable life.' She looked up at the pathologist. 'Thank you, Stewart. He looks perfectly normal for his ex-wife to identify him, and I appreciate that whether she does or not.'

Adam and Debra headed back to the station without speaking, both deep in thought. Debra's thoughts went along the lines of Barker looking so normal, just... dead. Adam's thoughts were along the lines of why now? Why had he done it now? The awful part of it was that nobody would ever really know because he hadn't left much of a note to explain anything.

Debra's phone pinged as they walked across the car park, and she saw it was some sort of response to the text she sent earlier to Angela Barker. She read it quickly – there were very few words to read – and confirmed that Philip Barker had no parents and no siblings.

Adam sighed. 'That's rubbish, really. No wonder he relied so heavily on alcohol. Once Angela threw him out he had nobody, except the pub and apparently three domino-playing mates. Not much to show for a life.'

'We need to go and speak to them, his friends. Maybe they knew something we don't know.'

'There's no rush, this isn't part of the remit of Major Crimes, it's a self-inflicted death.'

'But he's the stepfather, father really, of our victim.'

'You bullying me?'

She grinned at him. 'Sometimes you need a bit of bullying. No, it's more a sort of unease. Tell you what, I'll nip over tomorrow lunchtime to the Brown Bear, see if I can catch any of them in. That landlady's been helpful, so she'll point them out to me if they're in. Then I promise I'll let it go if we find no new info from the trip over to Chesterfield.'

Adam went into his office and opened up his computer. Stewart had sent him the full post-mortem report alongside the toxicology results, and he wanted to study them in peace. He had viewed the scene and hadn't doubted for a minute that it was a suicide, but the DI in him had to have it confirmed. And it was. Multiple drugs were present, as had been evident from the numerous packets, mostly empty, lying around the bedroom.

'What the hell caused this decision, Philip?' he asked quietly. 'Did you have anything at all to do with the death of Lucie?'

He leaned back in his chair, deep in thought. Would Barker have known Lucie was going to Midnight Mass? Would he have guessed it was the church nearest to the home she still shared with Angela?

Lucie wasn't a regular churchgoer, that much they did know. It had been a sudden decision, according to Angela, and in view of what Philip had done to her, Adam couldn't imagine any sort of conversation between them where she would tell him she was going to that particular church at midnight.

And Philip had been roaring drunk, hardly able to walk. Adam stood and looked out into the main office. 'Vicky,' he called. 'Did you contact Chesterfield taxi companies?'

Vicky was on the phone and she waved a hand to acknowledge she had heard him. She finished speaking, disconnected, and stood.

'That was the last one,' she said. 'It's a big one, so they had to go back and check lots of call-outs for Christmas Eve. They're emailing me a complete listing of all calls for that night up to 1am Christmas morning. But nobody, and I think I found them all, big and little businesses, had a call-out to a Philip Barker, or his address. I'll do a report and file it now I've done them all.'

'Thanks. Good job, Vicky. I honestly didn't expect him to have rung for a taxi, going by what the landlady of the Brown Bear said. She said he could hardly walk. I'm just clearing up oddments here, because I don't actually suspect Philip Barker of doing anything that could link him to this murder, but we have to rule him out officially. Let's just tidy it up completely by asking the ANPR lads to run his car number plate through the system between 11pm Christmas Eve and 2am Christmas Day. I'm sure that's just another box to tick, but it needs ticking.'

Vicky nodded. 'Will do. I'll let you know as soon as I have an answer.'

Adam returned to his office, a smile on his face. When Vicky had first joined his team she'd been like a little mouse, scared to join in with any banter, very quiet and just did whatever was asked of her, but now she had become possibly the most reliable member of Major Crimes, and he included himself in that. He also knew her full report on taxi firms in Chesterfield would be uploaded to the file within half an hour, ready for them all to inspect if necessary.

He felt oddly pleased that they were ruling out Philip Barker. He hadn't particularly liked the man, but it was the thought that he had been a father to Lucie for most of her life, and he couldn't imagine her dad killing her.

What wasn't pleasing him was that nobody seemed to be in line to be ruled in. He grinned to himself when he thought it seemed to be turning into an Agatha Christie novel where the vicar had done it. Except this vicar was a genuine bloke who had been deeply upset as the events had unfolded. Okay, he had known the victim's mother many years ago, but what sort of motive did that give him for killing Lucie? He'd only met her for the first time ever some forty-five minutes earlier. And quite apart from everything else, he liked Steve Rainforth.

He knew he was pacing, but he went back out into the main office. Debs had disappeared, and he hoped it was to make them a coffee. 'Any news from any of the lads?' he asked Vicky.

'No,' she said, 'but ANPR pulled their fingers out. No sign of that registration plate at all on Christmas Eve.'

'Good. We've more or less ruled him out as a suspect completely. You got a party booked for tonight?'

She laughed. 'I'm staying in with my mum. We stay up till midnight, sing "Auld Lang Syne", then go to bed, but we have a bottle of wine between us, and I make us a buffet meal. It's the same every year.'

'No dad?'

She shook her head. 'I've never had a dad. I remember Mum once having a boyfriend, lasted about three weeks and she got fed up with him. Too serious, she said.'

'I like the sound of your mum. Seems she knows what she wants from life. So, bugger off home now, you've done enough today. Go and enjoy your evening, and we'll make it a nine o'clock start tomorrow instead of seven.'

Her smile lit up her face. 'Thanks, boss. And tomorrow we'll go through all the reports from the congregation members that the lads have visited today. Let's hope something interesting comes from that.'

CHAPTER SEVENTEEN

Steve pulled Jenna to him and kissed her. 'Happy New Year, my love,' he said. 'This is definitely going to be our year. By this time next year we'll either have a new baby, or be very close to giving birth.'

He felt Jenna shudder. 'Nothing's certain, Steve. They may say the one ovary I have isn't working properly, and that we'll never have our baby. There are all sorts of things that could go wrong.'

'That's being defeatist. There's no guarantees with anything – it might be me who can't have children. But whatever happens we can always follow the adoption route.' He hugged her again. 'We will have our child, I promise you.'

She smiled. 'You're so right for me. You can always make me feel better when the world feels against me. Just ignore me, I'll get over it. I think I'm feeling down because of what we've had to go through this Christmas with that young woman.'

Steve took a deep breath. 'Let's not call her that young woman. She had a name, Lucie Barker. I don't think they're getting anywhere with it. I'm pretty sure Adam would have contacted me if they'd had a breakthrough. I'll maybe give him a ring tomorrow, see if they're any closer to solving who did it.'

They held each other tightly as they watched London join hands for 'Auld Lang Syne', and when was over they carried the empty food dishes and their glasses through to the kitchen.

'Let's leave them till tomorrow,' Jenna said. 'I think I'd like to simply slide into bed by my lovely husband and drift off to sleep in his arms.'

He laughed. 'That can be arranged. And, my precious one, it will be a happy new year.'

Adam and Elise had allowed the boys to stay up until midnight, their first time witnessing the madness that is New Year's Eve in the United Kingdom. William and Alfie, at nine years of age, were suitably impressed.

'Can we go to London for it next year?' Alfie asked. His brother nodded in agreement.

'I think not,' their father said. 'It's much cheaper to watch it on television, and a hell of a lot warmer.'

'If we're good all year, can we go?' Alfie was persistent.

Elise creased up in laughter. 'That's a step too far, Alfie. I reckon you two could only last one full day without being naughty, so let's not get giddy and make silly promises. Not on New Year's Eve anyway. That's a time for resolutions to be made that you're supposed to keep all year. It's an impossibility that you two could be good for an entire twelve months.'

'Boys, your mother has no faith in you.' Adam pulled them close. 'Come to think of it, neither do I. Be good for a full year? Not an earthly.'

'And that's it,' Elise said. 'It's bedtime now. You've enjoyed your first grown-up New Year?'

Both boys simultaneously punched the air with their fists. 'Fantastic,' Alfie said.

'Awesome,' William echoed.

'Right. Upstairs, teeth brushed extra hard after drinking Coca-Cola all night, PJs on and into bed. I'll be up in ten minutes.' Elise smiled as both of them groaned, and Alfie opened his mouth to plead for something until his mother held up a finger. He acknowledged defeat, and the two boys climbed the stairs.

Adam grinned. 'I could do with you in the office controlling my team. You did that with just one finger.'

'They understand that means no more arguing. I'm dreading them becoming teenagers. Shall we have another glass of wine now it's become a bit more civilised?'

'You go and say goodnight to the boys, I'll see to the wine. Anything to eat?'

She thought for a moment. 'Cheese and crackers?'

'Just what I was thinking.' He headed for the kitchen, and heard Elise going upstairs. It had been a brilliant night, with them playing bingo again until the television became more about New Year's Eve. They had then packed the game away and settled down to let the new year in traditionally. He reflected on how much the boys had grown up over the past twelve months – the previous New Year's Eve had been so different. They had allowed them to stay up, but by ten o'clock both were fast asleep.

He put some cheese and crackers on a plate, got out a couple of smaller plates and two fresh wine glasses, then carried the loaded tray through the lounge. He chose a Sauvignon Blanc, telling himself to remember he had to drive to work in just over eight hours and they'd already had a full bottle.

He could hear giggles and threats from upstairs, but eventually Elise made it back to him.

'They're bouncing,' she announced.

'They'll sleep in tomorrow morning. And they're bouncing because of the Coke they've been drinking.' He handed her a glass of wine. 'Happy New Year, my love.'

'Happy New Year, Adam. And get that murdering bastard found who killed that lovely young lass.'

Debra wished Dave a happy New Year at three o'clock in the morning as she handed him some paracetamols. She had been in bed since ten o'clock, after checking Kara was asleep, but Dave had such a dreadful cold he hadn't been able to hold up his head, so she resigned herself to an early night.

Now feeling fully awake she went back downstairs, opened up her laptop and began to read the reports filed by all the uniforms who had been out interviewing the congregation members. She got halfway through before closing it down, made herself a hot chocolate and headed back to bed.

She set her alarm for half past seven, recognising it would be better for Kara to go to her nan's for the day. Dave wasn't fit enough to look after a cat, let alone a child.

It was a disturbed night, fuelled by Dave's coughing and barking and intermittent fireworks exploding until around five o'clock, but she finally dropped into a deep sleep.

Debra got Kara ready, who was more than excited to be going to Nan's house, and left a note by the side of Dave's head, hoping he would see it. He might just panic that their beloved daughter wasn't there.

She headed into work after watching Kara disappear into the warmth and love of Nan's little cottage, and realised she was the first to arrive.

By the time everyone was in she must have said happy New Year twenty times. Adam looked a little worse for wear, but he walked straight to the front, yelled 'Happy New Year' and disappeared into his office.

She knocked on his door and popped her head around. 'You okay?'

'I blame Elise,' he said.

'Ah, drop too much then, and you didn't know how to stop.'

'I'll be okay in an hour. Just give me time.'

'I'll drive today, and I'll go get you a coffee.' She closed his door and headed into the tiny kitchen.

Adam opened up his computer and began to read through the assorted reports already uploaded by the teams who had spent the previous day speaking to anyone who had been in the church for Midnight Mass. There were five people who hadn't been interviewed; they would have to have a second visit in a couple of days.

It seemed at first glance that almost everybody had noticed the stranger sitting at the back on Roger's pew. But that was basically it. She had been one of the first to leave the church after the end of the service, so nobody had spoken with her, other than Roger.

Adam studied Roger Carson's report with a little more intensity.

> I did not know the young lady, did not get her full
> name, but she told me she was called Lucie. She was very
> quiet. She knew the carols we sang, but did not seem to be
> fully conversant with the routine of the church, especially
> for taking Holy Communion. She had a beautiful singing
> voice. I asked if she had been confirmed and she said not

*yet. She said she wouldn't go to the front, but I explained
she could have a blessing even though she couldn't take
Communion. We went to the front together, Reverend
Rainforth blessed her, and she helped me to stand from a
kneeling position before returning to the back pew. We
were the first to leave the church, she thanked me for my
help and we wished Reverend and Mrs Rainforth, who were
waiting in the porch, a happy Christmas. I headed off down
the path after wishing Lucie a happy Christmas, and she
seemed to be unsure which way to go. I stopped at the
bottom of the path for a minute to make sure she was okay,
but she didn't go home that way. I returned home without
seeing her again. She was a lovely, very pleasant young
lady, and I wish I could be more help.*

Adam reread the report, hoping he was missing something,
but the only thing he picked up on was that Lucie had
responded with 'not yet' to Roger's question about her being
confirmed. Had she been planning on going to church on a more
regular basis? That particular church was the closest one to her
home, so maybe she had felt the need for the comfort it could
provide. He must remember to ask Angela if Lucie had spoken
about it to her.

One other thing he had picked up on from Roger's
statement was that she hadn't left the church immediately, and
definitely hadn't followed him down the path to the road. Had
she stayed in the churchyard? Why?

Did she know of her mother's previous relationship with
Steve Rainforth? He pulled a notebook towards him.

*Questions for A
1 Was Lucie planning on starting to attend church
regularly?*

2 *Had she mentioned she might meet somebody after church?*

3 *Did L know of A's previous relationship with SR?*

His writing was a little wobbly, and he smiled as Debra brought in a coffee. 'No more alcohol till Easter,' he vowed as she placed the mug in front of him. She also gave him a glass of water and two paracetamols.

'Take these now,' she said. 'We have plans for today?'

'Not today, but tomorrow I want Angela to identify Philip, and then I want her bringing back here. We need to get this woman talking, find out what she's not saying. I suggest you ring her and make arrangements to pick her up tomorrow, she might just start to talk, woman to woman. Don't forget to notify the morgue when you know what time you'll be there. Maybe this afternoon we'll go to the church if I've recovered from this bout of flu.'

'Flu! Ha!' She grinned at him.

'You seem remarkably... sober.'

'I've got a husband with actual man flu, so I've been awake most of the night listening to him cough and I had to get up at the crack of dawn to wake Kara and get her over to her nan's for the day. Dave really isn't capable of looking after so much as a budgie at the moment, so alternative arrangements have been made.'

Adam groaned. 'And I'm not helping.'

'You'll feel better when we've been to church; everybody does, so I'm told.'

'We'll go to the churchyard first. Now everything is cleared away I want to stand where Lucie must have stood, see what she could see, because she would have dropped onto that gravestone instantly when her throat was slashed. Can we count Christmas and the New Year completely over now? I'm so fed up of the whole country being incommunicado. It's made everything so much harder. I'm booking a holiday for next Christmas.'

'Just drink your coffee and sober up. You'll not be so grumpy by the time we get to church. Wait while I tell Dave I've been to church, he'll crease with laughter. You could possibly have found a cure for man flu, DI France.'

CHAPTER EIGHTEEN

S teve Rainforth felt that strange sort of shock when you open the door and the man standing in front of you is the man you've been thinking about contacting all morning.

'Well, knock me down with a feather,' Steve said with a laugh. 'I've been wondering if I should contact you all morning, or whether I should wait till tomorrow when the world does a reset to how it used to be before Christmas.'

'You wanted something?'

Steve held the door open. 'Come in, I'm sure we can manage to put the kettle on.'

Debra and Adam walked down the hallway and into the kitchen, where Jenna was weighing out some flour.

Debra smiled at her. 'That looks lovely. I wish I could bake.'

'I quite enjoy it, but to be honest I'm trying to take my mind off everything else, because we keep saying "after Christmas" and now it is. We start IVF treatment shortly, and if it doesn't work... well, that thought runs through my mind all the time. All of these things on top of a murder in the churchyard have turned me to baking scones.'

SILENT NIGHT

'I'll make us a drink,' Steve said and he kissed his wife's head lightly as he passed her. He knew how scared she was, not of the tests, but of the results.

Adam and Debra sat at the table, and Jenna covered up her baking bowl and put it to one side. She joined them and Steve produced three teas and a coffee – Adam was still needing a lot of caffeine.

'You wanted to contact me?' Adam looked at Steve, who definitely didn't look hungover. 'Happy New Year, by the way.'

Steve laughed. 'I must have said that a hundred times this morning, and I only went for a walk in the woods. Happy New Year to both of you, and my earnest wish is that you solve this mysterious death in our churchyard as quickly as possible, and the killer is dealt with properly.'

'That's my earnest wish as well,' Adam conceded. 'But I feel as though we're no further on than we were a week ago. We've had the death of Lucie's father thrown into the mix now, although there doesn't seem to be any doubt that it was suicide. I just... oh, I don't know. I just want to know why. What drove him to it at this particular point in his life, and does it have anything to do with Lucie's death? I don't mean he was involved in it, but it had to have been a dreadful shock to him. To all intents and purposes, she was his daughter.'

'I shall keep him in my prayers alongside Lucie. Is Angela handling everything okay?'

'You haven't spoken to her?' Adam took a sip of his coffee.

Steve shook his head. 'No, I kind of feel I'm in a difficult situation with Angela because I know her. Or I did know her many years ago. I don't want her to feel awkward so I've not contacted her, but I also didn't know if she'd been formally interviewed or anything, so thought I wouldn't approach her until I'd heard from you. Hence my thinking about everything this morning, including my contacting Angela.'

Debra frowned. 'I can appreciate your problem, but in a way you're in a similar situation to us. It's your job, first and foremost. You could reach out to her, even if it's just an initial phone call. However, don't do it tomorrow, we're taking her to identify Philip Barker. She's not happy about it, but it seems Philip has no parents and no siblings, so she has reluctantly agreed to do it. She was going to drive in herself, but I'm going to pick her up because we want her in the station to answer a few questions. Nothing major, but she volunteers nothing so we have to ask.'

Steve felt a little sick. Since Ange's words to him as he left her home in the early hours of Christmas Day, he had known at some point it would have to come out that he was Lucie's father. And he didn't doubt the relationship for one minute. He had been keeping an appointment diary for years and remembered exactly when Angela had walked away from him. One week later he was in training to be a vicar. He'd even confirmed his beliefs by using the calculator on his phone. Yes, he was the father of Lucie Barker.

At this moment in time only he and Angela knew this. He had to speak to her, to find out what she intended doing. Would she keep it a secret between the two of them, or would she tell all to the pushy DI Adam France? Steve guessed if Adam wanted information he wouldn't stop until he had it.

So he had decisions to make. Should he make the first move and tell Adam, or should he do his normal trick of burying his head in the sand, hoping it would never surface?

And what of Jenna? If anyone had the right to know, it was her. He would be having tests to see if he could father a child, and yet he already had. And how would Jenna feel knowing he already had a child he had known nothing about?

His thoughts began to overwhelm him, and he shook his head. He needed to know what Adam and Debra were planning, in case he had to take steps first. He sipped at his tea and switched his attention to what they were saying.

'We actually came to tell you we've spoken with most of the congregation from Christmas Eve, with very little in the way of anything that could move this case forward. We've five that weren't at home yesterday, but we'll speak to them as soon as they return home. Your organist, Marjorie, wasn't in. Is she away for long?'

'She said she was being picked up immediately after the service, and would be back for the 5th of January service, so I don't know when she's actually going to be home, but she'll be here this Sunday in church. She went to stay with her daughter for the entire Christmas period.'

'Thank you. I guessed you might know her whereabouts. We've put a note through her letter box asking her to call the station as soon as possible, so we'll have to have some patience. Just when you think Christmas is over and done with...' Adam grumbled.

'Ignore my boss,' Debra said with a laugh. 'He's not well today. He'll be okay tomorrow after a good night's sleep.'

'I'm okay today,' Adam said. 'I just don't think it's necessary for everybody to talk.'

'You want us to have a séance?' Steve grinned. 'I've never organised one, but I can try, then you won't have to listen to anyone except spectral beings.'

'Now you're taking the piss, Reverend Rainforth. You allowed to do that?'

Steve shrugged. 'Dunno, never asked, but I'm allowed to do pretty much whatever I want as long as I've got this on.' He touched his clerical collar.

'Really?' Adam looked impressed. 'Perhaps I'm in the wrong job. I could do with a couple of days of doing whatever I want, with no consequences.'

'I didn't say there'd be no consequences,' Steve said, raising his eyes to the heavens.

'Ah, got it.' Adam grinned at the man he was beginning to appreciate – he had a wicked sense of humour, and was quick with repartee. 'You answer to a much higher authority than the Chief Constable, am I right?'

'Definitely right. You try explaining to God in front of that cross in church with Jesus, his only son, nailed to it, just why you've been unable to carry out his orders, or even his suggestions, and see how you feel then.'

'I'll stick to the Chief Constable, I think,' Adam responded. 'I just hope I don't see him, or even my DCI, today before I've had chance to stop my head from pounding. It's starting to feel better than it did at seven o'clock when my alarm went off. And I've no idea how Elise is feeling, I daren't ask her. It was my fault for suggesting one more glass of wine after we'd put the kids to bed. I promise I didn't mean one more bottle of wine.'

Steve and Jenna looked at each other and both burst out into laughter. 'You poor man,' Jenna said. 'I take it you don't drink very often.'

'At New Year,' Adam groaned. 'And really, it's only at New Year. The boys want us to take them to the London Eye next year. Think I might agree to that, then I can't drink.'

He finished his coffee. 'Thank you for helping to sober me up, that coffee was delicious. We have to get back now, see if anyone's managed to track down any of your errant congregation. We have statements from most of them, but nothing helpful. Nobody saw anything, not even Mr Carson who she was with for the entire service. He said goodnight, wished her happy Christmas and that was it.'

'Pretty much as Jenna and I did,' Steve said. 'I didn't even see which direction she went in after we had said goodnight to them both, although I did see Roger going down the path on his own.'

'Keep thinking, Steve. Some minor thing may occur to you, something you dismissed as irrelevant to anything at the time, but could be relevant now. We have absolutely no leads taking us to this killer. At one point I half suspected her father because of...' he hesitated. 'Well, just because, but he had an alibi of being unable to walk or stand up properly. He was legless, and we do have confirmation of that. We've also checked every taxi business in Chesterfield to see if he could have ordered a taxi, and we did an ANPR check on his own car, but he definitely wasn't out and about after he staggered home from the pub.'

Steve gave a gentle nod. 'I'm relieved to hear it. I would have found it almost unbearable if the man who had brought her up for over twenty years was the person who had killed her.'

'You do realise we have to look closely at her mother before discounting her involvement in it?'

'Angela? But...'

'No buts. It wouldn't be unheard of, and all we know is that she came to look for Lucie when she was late home. For some reason she didn't go to any officer and ask what was going on when she saw the police cars and forensic vehicles, she simply turned around and went back home. She says she didn't want to know if it proved to be her daughter who was involved, so she ignored it, but then we turned up, Steve, and she knew without us having to say very much at all. Remember?'

Steve nodded. 'How could I forget. I hope I never have to do anything like that again. I just felt that as it happened at my church it was right I accompanied you, but I promise you, that will never happen in any part of my future.'

'Well, if it's any help, I believe you were a comfort to Angela Barker that night. She started by wanting to blame you, as God's representative on earth, but it kind of switched around and she began to accept what we were saying.'

Adam stood. 'Thanks for the chat. We have to get back, see what everybody's up to, and try to figure out where we go from here. And if you hear from Marjorie, tell her we'll see her Monday.'

Steve went with them to the door, and watched as they walked down to their car. A good copper, he felt, and an equally good sidekick.

It was only as they drove into the station car park that Adam remembered his plan to go and stand where Lucie had died and just simply look. And feel. Tomorrow, when his head was better, they would do it. He didn't understand why he felt it was necessary, but it was. Tomorrow.

CHAPTER NINETEEN

'Yes, that's him. That's Philip Barker.' Angela turned from the viewing window and walked away. 'Am I done now?'

'Not quite,' Debra said. 'I have to take you to the station to complete your statement. Anyone who's been interviewed has to eventually agree that everything they have said is the truth – it's a legal thing, so DI France asked me to take you back with me before I run you home. Thank you for doing this.' She waved her hand towards where Philip Barker was being put back onto his refrigerated shelf. 'I know you didn't want to.'

'Too damn right I didn't want to. And the funny thing is I used to love him so much. He came into my life at a time when I needed a friend, and he became so much more. It wasn't instant love, but it grew to proper love as the years went by. Do you understand what I mean?'

'Oh, I do. And I'm sorry you lost that love, especially in the way it finally disappeared altogether. Alcoholism is a disease. When it really attacks a body, it's hard to handle it, and Philip clearly didn't try. I've a friend who never misses an AA meeting, he's too afraid of taking that one drink and sinking back down.

He knows it's a lifelong commitment, but he daren't even have one drink. Philip lost everything through it, because I'm sure when he raped Lucie it was because he was so drunk he had no idea just how bad his behaviour had become. Ending your relationship with him was probably the smartest move of your life.'

They exited the building and headed back to Debra's car.

'You're saying everything I've thought for the last five years. What I can't fathom is why the change in him was so sudden. He was drinking maybe once a week, and then he was drinking constantly. And it happened over maybe three weeks.'

Debra put the car into drive and accelerated away. 'Did something happen to him at this time? Lose his job? Did somebody die that he was close to?'

'No, nothing I can put my finger on. And he couldn't lose his job, it was his own business. He had his own small building company, Barkers Bespoke Building Ltd., did classy one-off work, charged top rates, we had a good life. He ended up selling the lot to the lad who had been his foreman, because it was clear he was under the influence of alcohol while at work and they were losing customers through it. Philip decided he'd rather drink than work, so his bank account grew from the proceeds of the sale and his drinking increased.'

'You have a beautiful home. Did Philip do that?'

'Over several years, yes. He used it pretty much as a training ground if he set on any school leavers who wanted to learn a trade. He threw away so much through drink, but mainly he lost my love. I tried to shield Lucie from it, because he was her dad, but she was no fool. She tried to make sure I wasn't alone with him, because when he was really drunk he became violent, but that brought even greater worry as I was always scared he would hit her as well. There's so much relief in knowing he's dead, but if it proves he had anything to do with Lucie's death...'

'We'll be discussing this back at the station,' Debra said, turning to look at her passenger. 'But I can tell you we've ruled him out as a suspect. Actually, alcoholism ruled him out. He was too drunk on Christmas Eve to even walk, let alone travel from Chesterfield to kill his daughter, especially when he couldn't have known she was at that church.' She indicated to turn into the car park.

Debra escorted Angela into the reception. Angela didn't want to hand over her bag, but she was left with no choice. It was explained she would get it back as she left, but interviewees weren't allowed to take anything through to the interview room with them.

She also wasn't too happy when she heard the door lock engage. She slumped into the chair, hoping somebody would turn up with a drink of some sort.

They didn't.

Debra stepped into Adam's office. 'Happy January 2nd.'

'Piss off,' he responded.

'You're feeling better then?'

'I'm fine. And no, I'll never drink again. Especially not with my wife, it was all her fault.'

'Forced it down your throat, did she?'

'She did. Right, what you been up to? Are you late?'

'Not quite. I've been working since eight o'clock, collecting the lady who's waiting in interview room 2 to speak to us. We've got the identification out of the way, she confirmed it was Philip Barker, and we've shared an interesting conversation on the way back, so hopefully it's softened her up to talk to us on tape.'

'Good. Let's leave her there for a bit. I've been going through the reports of the conversations the lads had with the congregation. I've also added a report of our chat with the reverend and his wife from yesterday, just filling in all the boxes.'

'I like him,' Debra said. 'Smart bloke, doesn't push his religion, it's just there if you want it. And he's got a good sense of humour. Always liked that in a man.'

'Debs, I absolutely refuse to crack chicken that crossed the road jokes just so you'll like me.'

'Impossible anyway,' she said and walked out of his office, laughing all the way to her own desk.

Vicky came across from the other side of the room and perched her bum on Debra's desk. 'Need a break,' she said. 'We're getting nowhere with this, are we?'

'Doesn't seem like it,' Debs agreed. 'Any thoughts? Just chuck them at the rest of us if you have.'

'No, I haven't, and that's the problem. There's no vehicular checks, no suspect checks, no checks on anything that I know about. Tell me something new, Sarge.'

'Okay, find me anything, dodgy or spectacular, I don't really care, just find me anything on Barkers Bespoke Building Ltd. It used to be Philip Barker's business before he started to drink. He ended up selling it to his foreman. Sorry, I don't know the new owner's name.'

'On it,' Vicky said, removing her rear end from Debra's desk. 'I'll print it out for you and upload anything I find to the file, okay?'

'You know me so well,' Debra said with a grin. She liked to see a printout rather than read on screen – she could make notes and doodle her thoughts on a printout.

She put in a quick call to Dave, who didn't sound any better but insisted at least he could breathe without choking now. 'Thank God for Night Nurse,' were his words. She told him Kara was staying with her nan until Sunday, partly to alleviate any chance of her catching whatever her daddy had, and partly because Nan and Grandy were so much more fun than Mummy and Daddy.

She disconnected, realising it really was man flu, and maybe she should extend a little more sympathy. He still sounded dreadful, and it was actually a relief that Kara wasn't at home. He could take himself off to bed whenever he needed to, and didn't have to worry about a small, very talkative child.

She looked across to Adam's office. He was on the internal phone, and she hoped it meant something had shown up somewhere and a smart uniformed officer out doing interviews had solved the whole thing. She laughed to herself. *You're losing it, Debs. Have you ever had a case where something like that has happened?* She answered her own thought with *there's a first time for everything.*

Adam left his office and walked across to her. 'I'm being harassed,' he said.

'That's okay, you can handle it today. You've recovered. Who's harassing you?'

'The Super.'

'Oh. That's not good.'

'He wants answers. I told him we do as well. He was a bit snooty about that comment, so maybe I shouldn't have said it, but surely he doesn't think we're sitting on our arses doing nothing? We've had the major battle of the Christmas period and half the country being somewhere where they're not normally living. I've told him we're now fully staffed and working on it as a team, and we hope to have it cleared up very shortly. The murder of Lucie Barker is a priority. Do we?'

'Do we what? Hope to have it cleared up very shortly? Yes, we do, it's just that at the moment we don't really have a suspect.'

'Thanks. That's cheered me up no end. He's going to ring

me tomorrow to see what progress we've made from today's enquiries.'

Vicky approached with a couple of sheets of paper stapled together. 'This is what I've cobbled together doing it the easy way, Sarge, but now I'm going to delve further.'

'What's this?' Adam glanced over Debra's shoulder, trying to see what Vicky had produced.

'This is a follow-up to something the lady downstairs said to me this morning. Apparently Philip Barker was a master craftsman in wood, which is why Angela's house is so beautiful. He used their house to train apprentices, so everything was perfect. He owned a really thriving business until he stopped turning up for work, or was drinking on the job, and the business started to fail. Eventually, and I don't as yet know who suggested it, the foreman, who was his right-hand man, bought the business from him. I asked Vicky to do a bit of digging on it.'

The printout listed the company name and address, and the registration number as it was listed on Companies House. The Managing Director was a James Lucas and the website confirmed nine employees as of 2024.

'Okay, Debs, we need to go visit Mr Lucas. We'll have our chat with Angela, try and unlock her mouth, get her telling us whatever it is she's keeping from us, and go and see Mr Lucas.'

'You can't, boss.' Vicky tried to hide the smile because she could guess what he was going to say. 'It actually says on the website that the business is closed for the Christmas break, reopening sixth of January.'

'Is there only us working in this bloody country? Sixth of January? That's nearly midsummer!'

'Look, we can either wait until Monday and go first thing, or we can find his home address and go visit him now, but I can't see what help he's likely to give us so we might as well leave it until Monday,' said Debra. 'It's really a loose ends sort of contact. I'm betting he's had no contact with Philip since the sale of the business went through.'

'You're right, I know you are. It's just constant, isn't it? Everybody goes awol except the vicars of this country, and it's their busiest time of the year. And ours at the moment.' He glanced at the large clock with the deafening tick. 'We'll go down to Angela at eleven, that okay?'

'That's fine by me. And don't let your phone call from the Super upset you any more, we're doing our best and he'll just have to accept that.'

'My God, I love having a brave DS. You'll tell him that, will you?' He winked at her and went back to his office, taking the printout with him.

Vicky sighed. 'I'll print you another one,' she said, returning to her own desk.

CHAPTER TWENTY

'DI Adam France, DS Debra Jessop, Angela Barker present. Second of January 2025.' Debra logged them in, then read Angela her rights. She looked absolutely astounded.

'Here we go again with reading me my rights! I didn't realise you suspected me of murdering my daughter. Or is it my ex-husband I've killed? Or don't you know? I'm starting to feel like a proper criminal.'

'You finished?' Adam said. 'You know we have to do it, we told you the reason we had you in an interview room, so don't act surprised by it happening again. And don't shout at us, shout at the prime minister who's in charge of rules and regulations in this country.'

Angela shrugged. 'It just gave me a bit of a shock. And yes, I understand why, but I'm pretty sure I won't be giving you any clues because if I had a clue as to who did it, I'd be dealing with it myself. As you know. I've said it a couple of times.'

'We have to advise you that such an action would definitely be stupid, so just allow us to do our job, put the felon away for life, and get justice for Lucie. You going to prison won't help anybody.'

She didn't respond.

'Okay, Angela. First of all, thank you for your patience. We had one or two things to clear up before we could get down here. I've asked for some tea to be brought in, it shouldn't be long. And thank you for what you did this morning. I know it can't have been easy, following on so soon from viewing Lucie, but we can now put your ex-husband's death to one side and concentrate on Lucie. We can confirm Philip's death was self-inflicted.' Adam spoke quietly and firmly.

Angela nodded, still not saying anything.

'For the tape, Mrs Barker nodded.' Angela glanced at Debra, clearly wondering what had happened to the friendly police officer who had been with her earlier. She didn't sound too friendly now.

The door opened and a uniformed officer carried in a tray, complete with everything necessary to make a cup of tea. Debra thanked him, and stood to make them a drink, then handed them round. 'We can carry on, but feeling a bit more refreshed.' She smiled.

Adam sipped at his drink before speaking. 'So, we understand why you asked your husband to leave the marital home. Why didn't you report what had happened to the police?'

'Lucie said no. I was going to do it anyway, but she became even more upset. She said she was in far too much pain to have anyone do tests, and he was her father, and she didn't want him getting into trouble. She bundled all her bedding and her nightie up into a black bag and threw it in the bin. She wanted no evidence to be left, she just wanted to forget it. I kept the shop open just for sales, we cancelled all classes saying she was really ill with Covid, and needed time to recover.'

Debra spoke softly. 'What did you remove from that black bag?'

Angela's face drained of all colour. 'Her nightie.'

'Do you still have it?'

'It's in a sealed plastic bag in my loft. But you don't need it now, any more than I do. I kept it for insurance.'

'Did Philip know?'

'Yes. He didn't know where it was because I said it was in a safety deposit box at the bank, and if he ever spoke to either Lucie or myself I would retrieve it and take it to the police.'

'Did Lucie know you still had it?'

'No. She believed it went to the tip with the bedding. She actually stood at the window and watched the bin men empty our bin, and then she said "that's it, it's over".'

'We'll send somebody with you when Debra takes you home, to recover that nightie. Obviously we won't be using it as evidence, possibly won't even test it, but it needs admitting to our evidence department as it does form part of our investigation.'

Angela nodded. 'I'm fine with that. I'd considered destroying it, but... well... I didn't, and that's it.'

Adam opened his folder and took out a small piece of paper. His questions. 'Okay, Angela, not much more and we'll have you taken home. Can you tell us if Lucie was planning on attending church regularly, or was this a one off because it was a special service purely for the celebration of Christmas?'

'She became interested in the church when...' she hesitated, 'when a leaflet was pushed through the door, showing the Christmas services. That was when I realised Steve was the vicar at our local church.'

'And that leads me to my next question. Did Lucie know you had enjoyed a relationship with Reverend Rainforth at one time?'

136

'I didn't tell her. I can't imagine she would know. Why?'

'Just checking. It may be relevant.'

'It wasn't relevant enough for me to say anything to her.' Angela was starting to snap back to his questions.

'When she said she was going to Midnight Mass, did she mention she might meet somebody, either there or after the service?'

'Not at all. She actually said she would be home by half past twelve at the latest. I was uncomfortable about her walking, but she wanted to walk. It's not far, she had on a warm winter coat and boots, and it was really frosty. Just the sort of weather she liked.'

'So she really didn't know anybody there?'

'Not as far as I'm aware, and I truly believe she would have told me if she had been meeting someone. She wasn't a secretive girl, we had a very open relationship, chatted about anything and everything. And as I said, she thought she would be home by half past twelve, so it didn't leave her much time to see anybody, did it?'

'Thank you for being so open, Angela. Is there anything else you think we should know? Anything that could possibly be relevant to the case, would help lead us to Lucie's killer?'

She dropped her head as if in deep concentration. Then she looked up, her eyes flicking between the two detectives. 'I can't think of anything, but if I do, I have your number, DI France. I'll ring you.'

Adam nodded. 'Thank you. Debra will drive you home now, and we'll send one of our lads up into your loft to retrieve that nightie. As I said, I don't think we'll need to test it, but I can't leave it where it is in case we do need confirmation of what happened. Thank you again for your co-operation in this, it must have been hard to admit to saving the nightie. You have a loft ladder?'

She smiled. 'A bespoke loft ladder. It's like climbing the stairway to Heaven, it's so perfect. Made in the days when Philip would have done anything for us, and did. I miss the old Philip, very much, but I hate what he became. And seeing him on top of my daughter, with me barely able to function because of the drugs he'd put into my drink – he'd become a monster. I did my duty this morning, but don't ask me to do another thing for him, because the answer will be no.'

All three of them stood and Debra took Angela back to reception, where her bag was returned to her. They were joined by Simon, a uniformed PC, who sat in the back seat of Debra's car as they travelled the couple of miles to Angela's home.

The loft ladder was exactly as Angela said – an immaculate, beautifully carved hand rail that folded in conjunction with the treads. Simon went up into the loft, and gave a low whistle as he looked around. It had been fully fitted out, with storage on every wall. Following Angela's instructions he searched for a drawer three up from the bottom. Inside he found an IKEA plastic bag with a sealed top, and fabric inside it.

He went back to the opening and waved it at the two women. 'Is this it?'

Angela stared at it for a moment. 'Yes, it is.'

Simon turned around and descended backwards. 'That puts my loft to shame,' he said. 'Mine isn't even fully floored and you take your life in your hands if you venture up there. Yours, Mrs Barker, is a palace. It's stunning.'

Angela escorted them to the door and watched as they drove away. Another round of questions dealt with, but determination not to reveal who fathered Lucie was still so strong in her. She regretted telling Steve, but felt he wouldn't say anything; it had simply been a moment of sadness and weakness that had led to the doorstep disclosure. However, he hadn't even contacted her to discuss it, so she felt a little more confident every day that her secret would stay safely hidden.

She closed the front door, locked it securely and went through to the lounge. She'd had a bad day, evening was drawing in and it was only three o'clock, and she wanted to close her eyes just for a few minutes...

And then it was ten past six, and her neck felt stiff. She groaned as she moved, standing up slowly. She switched on the Christmas tree lights, lit a couple of candles, and went to get a glass of water. It tasted truly delicious with the addition of the cherry-flavoured ice cubes Lucie had made as part of their Christmas festivities.

She couldn't halt the tears, didn't know how to handle herself. They hadn't only been mother and daughter, they had been friends, sisters. And suddenly she couldn't bear the pain of a life without Lucie. She had held it together until this moment, and now the grief was overwhelming her.

She cried and cried and cried.

Debra arrived home, took one look at her husband and packed him off to bed with yet more Night Nurse and paracetamols, plus a cup of hot chocolate in the hope it would soothe him to a restful sleep.

She personally thought it was a waste of time, his cough was so bad. She picked up her phone, had a short chat with Kara who was clearly having a whale of a time at Nan and Grandy's house, and who seemed somewhat disgruntled at having to return home on Sunday if Daddy was feeling better by then. 'And if he starts to cough again, can I come back to Nan's house?' she asked.

'No, sweetheart, you have school next week. Nan doesn't

want to be doing school runs, and I'm sure Daddy will be much better by then.'

They blew kisses at each other over the phone and said night-night. Debs sank back into the chair, suddenly exhausted. It had been a long and tiring day, but also quite emotional having to deal with Angela Barker.

She had no idea where to turn next – she reckoned tomorrow's briefing needed to be a very open one, where they could all pool their thoughts and maybe come up with ideas they hadn't already covered.

She closed her eyes and relaxed. Should she sleep down here? But what if Dave became worse during the night and needed medical help? She forced her eyes open, poured herself a glass of milk and headed upstairs. After brushing her teeth gently in case she woke up too much with a tough brushing, she climbed into bed. Dave felt hot, but that could be down to the hot chocolate... and he began to cough.

She sighed and picked up her Kindle. Some nights, she thought, are just destined to be long ones.

CHAPTER TWENTY-ONE

It took twenty minutes to de-ice her car, and Debra felt really pissed off that it was so cold. She also felt pissed off at how little sleep she had managed, but above all else she felt really sorry for Dave.

She might have had a bad night, but he had endured a much worse one. And then suddenly, around six o'clock, he had a coughing bout, sank back onto his pillow and drifted off into a much deeper sleep than he had been able to manage for several nights.

She had stocked up his bedside table with medication, left him a flask of coffee and a couple of sandwiches on a cling-film covered plate and a large note that said she loved him and he'd to stay in bed all day and rest.

It would normally have been Dave de-icing her car for her on such awful mornings, and she hadn't enjoyed the experience – Friday mornings should be warmer than this, she decided. She knew it was an irrational thought, but her worries for her husband were knocking everything else off kilter. Rationality wasn't part of her vocabulary at the moment, and heaven help any smart arse at this morning's briefing.

There seemed to be a sense of relief around the briefing room that the third of January meant a cessation of all festivities, and everyone was talking with renewed hope about 'putting this one to bed'.

There was instant quiet as Adam entered the room. Debra thought he looked tired, and hoped he didn't have illness at home to contend with. When he began to speak it became apparent he'd spent quite a lot of the night dissecting the reports from the lads who had managed to interview most of the congregation.

'So, we have five left to speak to. Forget Marjorie Wilson, the church organist, she's away until Sunday so DS Jessop and I will go and have a chat with her on Monday. That should be good, because she'll be expecting us. The other four need contacting today if possible.' He pointed to two uniformed officers. 'You two, book out a squad car and go and see what you can do. If they're still not available on this second visit, leave them our standard card asking them to contact us as a matter of urgency. Highlight the matter of urgency words, then they'll know we're serious.'

He looked around the room. 'There are some houses not too far from the bottom of the church path. Some are across the road, and quite a few are down the side. We haven't had chance to talk to their owners yet, so the rest of you organise yourself into three teams and get out there collecting signed statements that tell us whether or not they saw anything strange going on, like somebody running away after they'd just slashed a young woman's throat.'

He coughed. 'Forget I said that, I'm bloody tired. I'm not being insensitive, I'm feeling frustrated because we're no further on than we were on Christmas Day. And it was a long night working through all those reports. So, to prove I'm not going to sit behind my desk and catch up on some sleep, a piece of information we do need to check out is that Philip Barker used to own an upmarket joinery business by the name of Barkers Bespoke Building Ltd. DS Jessop and I are going there on Monday when they reopen after their Christmas break. No guarantees we'll get anything from it because it now belongs to Barker's ex-foreman, but we can't ignore anything as we clearly still know nothing. Whatever anyone discovers today please upload all reports to the file by the close of day so I can spend tonight reading through them.' Finally he smiled. 'And thank you for putting up with my grumpiness. I'll have a coffee, see if it wakes me up. And don't go knocking on doors till after nine, people could still be in bed. If anyone wants a bacon sandwich and a hot drink before they go out on this bloody cold morning, tell the lady on duty in the canteen to keep a list and I'll pop in and pay it later.'

There was a general cheer and a round of applause as Adam walked back into his office. Debs followed him. 'One–nil to you. Thought you'd lost them at one point, but bribery by bacon butty is always a winner.'

'They're a good set, never argue, just get on with it.'

'I know, and they're feeling as frustrated as we are. I feel absolutely no hope that we'll get anything from the remaining five congregation members, and then we really have reached a dead end. I feel so guilty when we come into contact with Angela Barker. She always looks at us as though we have something to tell her, but...'

'We really don't,' Adam finished her sentence for her. 'You want a bacon butty before we go?'

'Go where?'

'I still want to go back to the churchyard. I don't know why, so don't ask me, but two heads are always better than one, so they say, so your head can accompany my head. It's probably just to stand there and look, just get a feel for the place when it's being normal, without a body lying across a grave. That is the thing that's stopping me sleeping, seeing Lucie lying face down on that grave, already dead by the time Steve and Jenna got to her.'

'We've seen lots of dead bodies. Do they all affect you like this?'

Adam shook his head. 'No, and I think it's a combination of circumstances, time of year and her age. It feels as though it's haunting me. And you know something else that occurred to me while I was reading through all the reports? These people are Christians. It shines through their words, and our lads have written down what they said verbatim. Every one of them said they would pray for Lucie, and for Lucie's family. Every single person they interviewed said that.'

'You think their dedication comes from Steve leading them?'

'I don't think there's brainwashing involved, if that's what you mean,' Adam said with a laugh. 'No, I think the belief is already within them when they arrive at church. Steve is their guide, their teacher, they turn to him when they need help or advice, and they listen to everything he says. If anybody chose the right career it was him. And Jenna seems the perfect partner. I really like both of them.'

'So should we tell them we're going to stand in their churchyard?'

Adam frowned for a moment. 'No, I'd rather they didn't know. Just the two of us should do this. I want to simply stand, not talk for the sake of talking, but comment if we feel or see something relevant. The crime scene tape and the tent might have been removed, but it is still a crime scene. We may feel nothing, it all may be a complete waste of time, but it will be crossed off my list.'

'So back to your original question. Shall we have a bacon butty and a coffee before we go? I can nip down and get them.'

'When did you last eat?'

She thought for a moment. 'Cornflakes, yesterday morning.'

'Mine was Weetabix yesterday morning. Yeah, two bacon butties and two coffees added to my bill. I'll give the bank a ring and organise a loan to pay for this lot, I think.' He laughed.

Both Adam and Debra felt better for the food, and Debra said she would drive because she needed to call in at home for a minute after they had finished at the church.

'You're worried?'

'I am. He's not a person who's ever ill, or at least never admits to it, but this has floored him. I did a Covid test but it was negative, so it appears to be a winter flu. But it's a stinker, I'm telling you. I'm so relieved my mum and dad have taken Kara until Sunday, but she has to come home then because she's back at school on Monday. So if you don't mind, I'll just pop in, check he's okay, and we can go back to the station after.'

'No problem, and if he needs an ambulance, send for one. If it's that bad it could turn to pneumonia.'

Debra drove up the twisting lane that led to the pretty church and pulled up outside the gate. There were no other vehicles around, although they could see Steve's car parked on his driveway.

They walked a few steps up the path, then stepped off to head towards the spot where Lucie had taken her last breath. Some attempts had been made to remove the blood, but not successfully.

'We have to sort this,' Adam said. 'Some relative may well visit this grave and it won't be good if there's bloodstains on it. Do we have a gravestone cleaner in our contacts?'

'I'll find somebody when we get back. Fortunately Emily Rowbotham died in 1852, so I doubt she'll have visitors unless some smart alec is doing a family tree. But you're right, the blood does need removing.'

'Right,' Adam said, his voice firm, 'let's set up this scene. It says on the PM report that the cut went across her throat from left to right. She fell forward onto the grave, banging her head in the process, although that didn't contribute to her death. Stand here, Debs,' he said.

She moved to where he indicated. He pointed his phone at her as if it was a knife and gently pretended to cut across her windpipe.

'Now react.'

Debra twisted away and fell towards the grave, holding out her hands to land them on the top of the headstone.

'Whoever it was stood in front of her. I believe she would have tumbled backwards if her attacker had slashed her from behind. But why was she here? Did she just pick a random place to wait?'

'To wait?'

'Oh yes. I'm not saying she was waiting for a person to meet up with them, but she was waiting for something. There's absolutely no reason for her to be in the depths of the graveyard in the early hours of Christmas morning. Just bear with me, Debs, while I turn you into Lucie.'

He moved her so she was standing by the side of Emily's grave facing the entrance to the church, which was some fifty yards away. 'Right, that's how I feel she was standing, waiting. Now, I want your genuine reaction. You have to imagine I'm the killer.'

Debs nodded, hoping he wasn't. This all felt very spooky. She waited for further instructions.

'Hello.'

She instinctively turned towards the sound of Adam's voice. He held up his phone once again, drew it across her throat and she staggered onto the grave, this time doing it properly and actually landing on the tiny gravel pieces.

Adam helped her up, and she dusted down her clothes. 'Thank heavens for washing machines,' she remarked, albeit a little sarcastically.

'Sorry, I needed genuine reactions. Her killer was already here. This is why nobody saw him coming up the path. He could have hidden behind one of the big headstones, because there's dozens of them, and slowly worked his way towards the spot she had chosen to wait at.'

'But it constantly brings us back to what or who she was waiting for. What did Lucie know that nobody else knew? And what was the real reason for her trip to this church? Was it really for a Midnight Mass, or was there some other reason?' Debra felt an angry pulse flood through her – did the woman take a risk that was completely uncalled for?

CHAPTER TWENTY-TWO

'Okay, come stand by my side. We're now Lucie. At our back is a killer that she knows nothing about. Okay?'

'Too many okays, but I'm with you so far. She's looking across to either the church doorway or the path everyone walks down to get home. The only other pathway leads directly to the garden gate of the vicarage.'

'Hold on to that thought. Right, so stand and look for a moment. Be Lucie. Talk me through what you're looking at as a woman.'

'You think I see differently because I'm a woman?'

'Well, I'd be looking at the architecture of the stone canopy above the door, at the intricate metal gates that are locked with a padlock that any self-respecting scrapman could break off in order to remove those superb gates – what are you looking at?'

'I'm looking at the end of an enjoyable service, I'm looking at people leaving, and I'm looking at a vicar locking the main door with a key, and walking down the steps to the metal gates. Then I hear "hello" behind me. End of story.'

'And that's the point when Steve heard a thud and a cut-off

scream. Was she... could she have been waiting to speak with Steve?'

'You think?'

He shrugged. 'According to Angela, she didn't know of any relationship from long ago, so why she would want to speak with him, I have no idea. Unless she wanted to discuss feelings engendered by being in church, but it was a strange time to do that.'

'We have to talk to Steve again, bring him to this spot, feel what we're feeling and seeing. But we need him away from Jenna, just in case she doesn't know about this early relationship when they were still kids, really.' Debra spoke while turning around, surveying the scene in front of her.

'I agree. Jenna runs a mother and toddler group in the church every Tuesday morning. Maybe we could accidentally visit Steve on Tuesday. She wouldn't even need to know then, unless Steve chooses to tell her.'

'Sometimes you're pretty smart for a man.'

'Touché. I asked for that after telling you to think like a woman.' Adam grinned at his partner. 'Right, let's just stand for a couple of minutes and let this scene sink in. Once again let's be Lucie, let's experience seeing whatever she was while waiting for whatever she was waiting for, and I'm becoming more and more convinced it was Steve. But what bothers me is that Steve doesn't see it. He's never once mentioned she could have been here for him. You know, Debs, we will get to the bottom of this. This won't descend into our cold case files. It's become too important.'

They stood side by side, both immersed in their surroundings. Both fully aware that there had been a dead woman on the grave they now stood at.

Adam stayed in the car while Debra nipped inside her house to check on Dave. There was no sign of him downstairs, so she went quietly up to the bedroom.

He was fast asleep, and she guessed he had remained asleep since she had left for work because nothing on the bedside table had been touched.

He was breathing easily, and she smiled. It was such a relief after the last few nights. She closed the door quietly and crept back downstairs.

Debra slid into the driving seat. 'He's asleep, and it's such a relief.'

'Good. You need to do a restock of anything for him before we go back to the station?'

'No, my kitchen's become a pharmacy. I think whatever's wrong must have peaked, he's breathing so much better, and he didn't even open an eye when I went in. We'll go straight back, see if anything has come in from our missing congregation people.'

Adam turned to her. 'What if – and this is just a what if – Steve was actually the one-night stand, and Angela's referred to him as that to throw us off the scent. He was with her twenty-five years ago, he could easily have been Lucie's father.'

She nodded. 'We think alike. It had crossed my mind a couple of times, but it's difficult to ask if one of them doesn't know about it, and I can't help thinking if Steve had known, he would have told us before now.'

Well, I'm pretty sure neither of them is going to tell us about it. It's a pity we don't have Steve's DNA on our database,' he said with a laugh.

'I don't think Steve has ever had so much as a criminal

thought ever, never mind done an actual criminal deed. He's definitely not going to be in our database.'

'We're going to have to be really careful, especially as they're starting IVF. Let's park this thought for the time being,' Adam said. It had been a strange afternoon and he was glad they had returned to where the murder had taken place. He closed his eyes for a moment, and opened them as they pulled into the car park.

'The men in my life seem to need sleep at the moment,' Debs said as she smiled at him. 'Don't read reports tonight, try sleeping instead.'

'I don't think I'll have much choice. My eyes keep closing on their own.'

'Well before you go to sleep, you'd better settle your canteen bill. I hear they did really well in sales of bacon butties this morning.'

Adam groaned. 'Don't remind me. I'll go do that now. You want a coffee while I'm there?'

'Yes please. It might calm my brain down, it's got all sorts of strange thoughts going through it. We're not working this weekend, are we?'

'The rest of the country doesn't appear to have returned to work yet, so no, we're having the weekend off unless something dramatic happens before we go home tonight. Deal?'

'Deal,' she said and got out of her car.

She watched as he headed towards the canteen, and grinned. This could definitely be a credit card purchase, she figured.

It was fairly quiet in the briefing room, despite it being full of people. Everyone looked in Debra's direction as though expecting some great news, but she just waved a hand and headed for her own desk.

Vicky strolled over. 'You dumped the boss?'

Debra smiled. 'He's gone to the canteen to pay his debts. We've been out to the churchyard, just looking and being still. Apart from him trying to slit my throat and bash my head on a gravestone that is. It's dangerous having Adam France for a boss. It was a good exercise to do though, in all fairness. Just talking it through led us down other possible avenues, but we're putting everything on hold until Monday, when we firmly trust the whole bloody country will be back at work.'

'We've got the weekend off?' Vicky looked suitably impressed.

'Yep, unless something dramatic comes through that door in the next half hour or so, I reckon we have. It's been so frustrating not being able to work properly because of Christmas family time, and that's basically what it is. And church people take it even more seriously than the rest of us.'

Vicky couldn't resist a laugh bubbling out of her. 'Could that be because it's nothing to do with Christmas trees and fairy lights, more to do with the birth of the Christ child?'

'Oh shut up. You know what I mean. Would you believe none of the four lads that visited today have arrived back home from visiting their relatives, or simply being on holiday? It's a pain, I'm telling you.'

Vicky walked away, still laughing. She rarely saw the grumpy side of Debra, but today it was showing. She opened her desk drawer, took out the packet of Rolos she had been dipping into all day, took two out and left the last one in the packet.

She returned to Debra's desk, and took hold of her hand, dropping the chocolate still in the packet into it. Debra gazed at it for a moment, recognised the significance of it, and burst into tears. 'See, I love my boss enough to give them my last Rolo,' Vicky whispered, and gave Debs a hug just as Adam appeared with the coffees he had been instructed to bring.

'Debs,' he said, 'go home. Now. Go and make sure he's okay, and if he isn't get an ambulance. If he is, make him some tea and toast. But go home. Vicky can have your coffee.'

Vicky removed Debra's jacket from where she had placed it on the back of her chair, and helped her put it on. 'Dave's no better?' she asked quietly.

'I'm hoping so, but the worry just overwhelmed me when you gave me the Rolo.' She turned to Adam. 'Thanks, boss. I'll ring you later if I have any problems, okay?'

'Make sure you do,' he said. 'And I definitely don't want to see you again until you're sure it's safe to leave Dave.'

Adam handed the spare coffee to Vicky. 'Enjoy it, I don't buy coffee for just anybody, you know.'

'You bought it for everyone today,' she pointed out. 'And you bought this for Debra, so it doesn't actually count against me because I got it accidentally.'

'Smart arse,' Adam muttered as he walked away. 'And there's no sugar in it.'

'Good job I don't take it then,' was her rejoinder.

Adam placed his coffee on his desk and leaned back in his chair. Debs crying! He felt quite shocked. It did occasionally happen, tears in the office – they covered some pretty brutal crimes – but it was usually Debra who was the one mopping up other's tears, not her own.

He felt as though he'd missed something, or maybe it was that she'd held back on how poorly Dave actually was. He'd talk to Elise about it when he got home, maybe take some flowers round on Saturday and see for himself how she was coping.

He opened his computer, saw there were no new filed reports, and literally gave up. This country needed to grow up and not be on holiday en masse. Christmas needed to become a spread-out holiday, not a period of frivolity and Christmas crackers squashed into a two-week period where people stopped doing everything.

Policemen had jobs to do, and they couldn't do them if there was nobody to talk to! He could feel his anger against the world growing by the second, and he knew it was because he felt so upset that he hadn't picked up on Debra's issues before they reached the tearful stage.

He was a bad DI, he decided. Although he had just spent a small fortune on bacon sandwiches and coffees for the troops, so he couldn't be bad all the way through, could he? But would he have thought of giving someone he loved his last Rolo? No he flipping wouldn't, he liked Rolos. Although maybe Elise might be the exception to that rule, maybe he could think about giving her his last one. But would Alfie and William then start to feel left out of the Rolo love-fest?

He closed down his computer, realised he'd removed his jacket down in the canteen and left it there, and walked out of the briefing room telling everyone to go home and not return – unless any other bodies were found – until Monday morning at seven. There was a universal clapping of hands, and a chorus of *thanks, boss* from various points in the room, and as he walked back down to the canteen he finally felt a smile creep across his face.

CHAPTER TWENTY-THREE

Debra arrived home feeling utterly drained. With a case that was seemingly going nowhere, a man with a close connection to their victim who had completed suicide as a possible way out of a terrible situation, and a truly poorly husband who wouldn't see a doctor she felt completely fed up and tearful.

She unlocked the front door, hung her coat in the cloakroom and went into the lounge to close the curtains and switch on the tree, possibly for the final time that year. The weekend would be spent turning her Christmassy home back into a normal one, and she couldn't wait.

Dave was on the sofa, nursing a mug of something warm. He smiled up at his wife. 'You're early, sweetheart. Don't tell me you're starting with this.'

She stared at the man who had coughed all the way through the night until he had finally hit exhaustion so deep his body had shut down into a really deep sleep.

'You're feeling better?'

'I ache a bit, and my chest feels sore, but in comparison to this time yesterday, I feel a hundred per cent better.'

'When did you last have some medication?'

'About an hour ago, but I'm feeling so much better. I'm not sure I could do a highland jig yet, but I'm getting there.'

'You've never done a highland jig.' Debra felt the tears from earlier begin to resurface. 'I cried at work.'

'What?' Dave looked horrified.

'Because of the case, because of you, and because Vicky gave me her last Rolo. And Adam threw me out, told me to go home and stay home until Monday. It's been such a frustrating time, everybody's away visiting relatives, or at Meadowhall for the sales, or just doing stuff because it's Christmas. And then I popped in at lunchtime and you were in exactly the same position, fast asleep, as I had left you in when I went to work this morning, so I hoped it meant that being able to sleep was helping you heal.'

'And it was. I hardly dared move when I finally woke up in case it triggered off a coughing bout, so I carried on lying in bed, but eventually I had to get up to go for a wee and I wasn't wobbling all over the place. I knew I'd turned a corner, but I'll continue the meds for the next couple of days. I know we joked about man flu, but this has been the worst thing I've ever experienced.'

'Did you try the sandwich I left?'

Dave shook his head. 'I didn't.' He held up his cup. 'This drink is from the flask, and it's totally delicious. I feel as if I've had nothing but water for days.'

She laughed, all stress gone now he seemed to be recovering. 'You have only had water for days. You think you could manage something now?'

He shook his head. 'I'm not hungry. I just needed a warm drink. And maybe somebody's last Rolo. I haven't had a Rolo for years, didn't even know they still made them.'

She walked around the sofa and, leaning over the back of it, she wrapped her arms around him, kissing the top of his head. 'I'll buy you a whole packet of them if it will make you feel well again. I was so worried, so scared it was going to lead to hospitalisation.'

'Is Kara still at your mum's?'

'Yes, I didn't want her coming down with this. We'll both FaceTime her tonight so she can see you're getting better.' She let go of him and stood up. 'And now I'm going to make a coffee because Adam threw me out and gave my coffee to Vicky.'

Dave looked at her, a frown creasing his forehead. 'What?'

'Don't ask. Everything's okay, and I'm under instructions to forget everything until Monday morning.'

Dave smiled at the woman he knew so well. 'Stupid instructions. Go get your coffee, and we'll talk through what you've been doing or not doing since I did my disappearing act. I promise to try to stay awake, but if I fall asleep it's not through boredom, it's because my body seems to have a mind of its own at the moment.'

'Understood. Be back in a minute.'

She entered the kitchen, and leaned her head against the fridge door, her eyes closed. If she believed in the God that everyone they had talked to recently believed in, she would be thanking him for the vast improvement in her husband. And just to be on the safe side, she did. 'Thank you, God,' she whispered.

She picked up the kettle, shook it, then put some water in it. She clicked it on, spooned some instant coffee into a mug and opened the fridge door. Milk or cream? No contest, she used the cream.

She carried her mug through to the lounge. Dave had pulled up his legs, laid his head on the cushion and closed his eyes. She smiled at the normality of it all, and returned to the kitchen, closing the lounge door behind her to keep the room warm.

She switched on her laptop, logged in with her police ID, and opened up the file dedicated to the murder of Lucie Barker.

She checked if any new reports had been uploaded, and saw there was one from Adam detailing their morning's visit to the churchyard. She read through it; the language was simplistic, didn't express any of the discussions they had enjoyed while there, with certainly no mention of being slashed across the throat by a mobile phone.

It made her smile, but she felt they had reached something while they had spent that time there, a sort of new understanding of where the case was heading, and she knew one day in the near future they would know what it was.

There were new reports from the teams still trying to clear up the list of congregation visits, but they had nothing to add because the targets still hadn't returned home from their Christmas breaks. The reports reminded her she needed to add stuff to her diary, so she went to the cloakroom where she had hung her bag alongside her coat, and collected the little blue book.

She flipped to January the sixth and entered Barkers Bespoke Building Ltd., followed by Marjorie Wilson. Maybe just one little snippet from either of these sources would be the lead they could follow to take this case to the conclusion they all wanted.

She pulled up the reports from the people already interviewed and started to read the newest ones, which were all from houses that were nearest to the church. She expected zero from these interviews. It had been Christmas Eve, not a time for watching what other people were doing.

Six people had been interviewed, with four homes still to visit due to no response the first time around. All six said the first thing they saw was a large number of police vehicles. They weren't aware of any activity prior to that, not even of worshippers leaving after Midnight Mass. It was quite a secluded area that had suddenly been enveloped in flashing blue lights and voices.

She read them all carefully, but nothing sent a tingle down her spine.

She moved on to the reports she had glossed over, the people who had attended the service and had already been interviewed. As she read she realised something; most of them called Lucie 'the young girl' and not 'the young woman' and almost everybody remembered her as the one who had the blessing and didn't take Holy Communion.

Steve himself remembered her in that same vein, so Debra decided Lucie must have wanted to keep in the background. It was probably Roger leading her to the front that had created the need for the blessing. 'I bet she would have simply sat at the back and just watched if it hadn't been for the old man,' she said quietly. But would that have affected the outcome? If she hadn't been made to mix, would she have left earlier and made it home without being attacked?

Or was this death always meant to be? Again she thought through the facts they already had. Lucie didn't make the decision to go until Christmas Eve. Did this mean the killer just picked someone at random? Did the killer have a thing against Christianity in general, and want to cause mayhem after such an emotional Midnight Mass. The reports all showed it had been an exceptional service. Or did the killer simply follow her, possibly from home, then wait knowing she would have to come out again?

Lucie hadn't helped herself if this was a random killing. Why didn't she simply go straight home? The timing of when the scream was heard meant she was waiting, lurking, in the graveyard, she hadn't even got as far as walking down the path that led to the road that would eventually see her arrive safely at her home. So could it have been a random killing?

Usually that would mean the killer would decide they'd enjoyed it, and go on to their next victim, but there had so far been no evidence of even an attempted attack. Debra couldn't shake the feeling she'd had from the start that it was targeted, not random, but if it was targeted, who the hell had done it?

Questions had been asked of the one person who should have known: Angela Barker. But she had been unable to come up with anyone who would want her daughter dead. Everybody loved Lucie.

She sat back, deep in thought. She felt as if she was simply regurgitating earlier thoughts, but she also acknowledged she was tidying up her mind. And going to that churchyard today had been the key to that. Adam's actions might have been unusual but they both had a greater understanding of the crime and how it happened. And she hoped that somehow on Tuesday they could speak with Steve Rainforth and find out if he knew why Lucie would be hanging around after everyone had left, if it wasn't to see and speak with him.

She picked up her cup – all this thinking was creating a thirst. It was her first sip and it was cold. She tutted in frustration, stood up and clicked on the kettle. She seemed destined not to get a coffee this afternoon, and that couldn't happen. She needed thinking time, and the caffeine would help with that. As would a piece of Christmas cake.

It did. The cake was rich and now the coffee was hot. She relaxed, staring at her screen before logging out of the session. Then she typed in *Barkers Bespoke Building Ltd.*

It would be good to try and get a feel for the place before they arrived on Monday morning for a chat.

James Lucas was a good-looking chap. On the website he was dressed in a smart suit, and he sported a huge smile. He was standing in front of the building that housed the company, and she credited him with some sense for keeping the original name of Barkers. She guessed Philip Barker had enjoyed an enviable reputation for excellence. She had seen his own home, the one he had created for his family before alcohol replaced people in his life.

She was looking forward to speaking to James Lucas – maybe they would learn more about the late Philip, and why he couldn't resist the lifestyle he chose. And just maybe Lucas would know a little more about Lucie, about the relationships within her family, and about how Philip felt about her knowing she wasn't his genetic child.

CHAPTER TWENTY-FOUR

Weekends begin with a lie-in, but Adam's began with him wondering why he was wide awake at six o'clock, hungry as a horse, and in definite need of caffeine in a big mug. The Christmas mug the kids had bought him would do nicely, thank you very much, he decided.

He popped a pod into the coffee machine, ran it through, then he put a second one in. It was a very large, two pod sized mug, and exactly what he needed. He opened the fridge to see what delightful treats were there that would satisfy a hungry man's appetite, and he spotted a new pack of bacon. He smiled. He might just manage a bacon and tomato sandwich, then he would decide what to do with his day.

Unless, of course, Elise had already decided what he should do with his day. He opened the bacon, placed two rashers on the grill, then added another one as a just in case. He justified the addition by thinking it was just in case three would be better than two. The cupboard revealed three tins of tomatoes, so he opened one and tipped the contents into the pan, giving it a bit of a mash with a fork before switching on the heat under the pan. The bacon was starting to sizzle, and he sat down with the huge Father Christmas mug that said *world's best dad* on it, and sipped slowly.

It was quiet upstairs, and as it was still dark he hadn't raised the blinds at the kitchen window. He wanted to enjoy the solitude for a little longer without allowing anything of the outside world into his life.

Ten minutes later his bacon sandwich, with all three rashers, was in front of him. He was about to take a bite when he heard speech. From Elise. 'My word, that looks good.'

He passed it to her and stood to put three more rashers under the grill.

'Adam France, you're my favourite husband.'

'That's good to know, favourite wife. Would you like a coffee as well?'

'That would be lovely. Yep, definitely my favourite.'

She took a bite of the sandwich and he watched with a small feeling of satisfaction as the tomato fell out and landed on her pink dressing gown. She looked down. 'Oh dear,' she said. 'Did you wish that on me?'

He handed her the newly brewed coffee with a smirk. 'Of course not, favourite wife. Do we have plans for today?'

'You're not working?'

'No, just find it impossible to stay in bed after six, it seems. Shall we take the boys out into the hills and let them run riot on the rocks?'

'We have options.'

He looked surprised. 'We do?'

'Yep. They need new shoes for Monday. We can either go to Meadowhall today, or we can go tomorrow. We can either go to Derbyshire today, or we can go tomorrow. Turn your bacon over.'

He followed her instructions. 'We'd best go today to get the shoes, I suppose, just in case we can't find any. Then at least we have another day to go further afield to find what they want. But if we get some today, we can do Derbyshire tomorrow for definite?' he asked.

'We can. That bacon is definitely sizzling.'

He sorted out his sandwich and sat opposite Elise, who was close to finishing hers. 'Lovely breakfast,' she said.

'Certainly is, and I'm going to eat mine before the boys get up and take it.' He took a bite and the tomato went down the front of his T-shirt.

Elise didn't even apologise for the explosion of laughter.

Alfie and William weren't a bit impressed by having to go shoe shopping, but when their mother explained to them that the only footwear that actually fitted them were the new slippers they'd had for Christmas, and did they really want to go to school in them, they admitted defeat.

As a result of all the assorted discussions, Adam was sitting in a coffee shop reading a newspaper and enjoying the ambience of the place. His wife was with their twins who would no doubt be arguing over which shoes to pick.

His own childhood had been one in which new shoes really were a luxury, and he always seemed to get his cousin's well-worn hand-me-downs. He felt a sense of happiness that he could afford shoes for his boys without having to think about it. It truly was a different world to the one he had endured during his early years.

He turned the page and folded it so it was comfortable to read. An article about the murder investigation being no further on was right in the middle of the page, so he smoothed it out to read it.

It was a good article, didn't tell lies, except possibly that the investigation seemed to have ground to a halt. He didn't agree with that, and after their short stint in the churchyard he felt there was something that was so close he could almost touch it, and knew that one day it would be so obvious they would kick themselves for not having seen it sooner.

The article made no mention of how difficult it is to take an investigation forward when half the country isn't at home, and just for a moment Adam wanted to pick up his phone and ring the editor, tell them how stupid their article was. He calmed himself down by considering they actually knew nothing of police work, the meticulous aspect of it where you had to be absolutely certain of all facts, because if you got anything wrong there was always some clever clogs lawyer happy to take you on.

He left the newspaper on the table, drained his coffee and walked outside. There was a bench close by, and he sat there, patiently waiting for the boys to find him. They would possibly be subdued by having to buy new shoes when they could have had a new game for the PS5 recently delivered by Father Christmas. He felt quite saddened by the obvious signs they were already querying the Santa lie, and knew this had been the last Christmas they would be able to use it. Life was so much more fun with a Santa Claus in it.

He rang Debs while he was waiting for Elise and the boys to find him, and she reported that Dave was much better, the cough was still there but not as bad, and he was sleeping himself well. He rang off, saying he would see her on Monday.

He spotted Alfie and William in the distance and waved to attract their attention. Within a minute they were excitedly telling him about the 'cool' shoes their mother had just bought them, and they removed them from the classy shoe boxes to show him. 'Super,' he said and raised an eyebrow at Elise.

'Don't ask,' she said, 'but if the bank manager rings you, I don't want to talk to him.'

They didn't stay much longer because he was dangerously

near the phone store, and his iPhone was looking a little worse for wear. If he went much closer to the shop his credit card wouldn't look too healthy either, so he steered the boys towards the Next store, which led them to the car park. Passing through the shop Elise managed to spot a dress and some shoes she could no longer live without, so by the time they were all strapped safely in the car, Adam was mentally, emotionally and fiscally exhausted.

'Shall we have a takeaway tonight?' Elise said. 'I really don't feel like making a meal after all this walking and stuff.'

'Explain stuff.'

'Spending.'

'So we'll spend a bit more having a takeaway?'

''fraid so.'

'Chinese?' Adam admitted defeat.

With the boys in bed, Gold radio playing via Alexa, and a glass of wine each, there was peace in the lounge. Adam was reading, Elise was sketching, trying out some new pens she had picked up in Meadowhall.

'I'm glad we've taken the tree down,' Elise said without looking up, 'but it has been lovely this year, hasn't it?'

'The tree or Christmas?'

'The tree, silly. Christmas hasn't been too good, you've been on a different planet. And I'm not complaining,' she jumped in quickly, 'because I know Lucie Barker's death has really got to you. I know you try not to bring work home, but I am here for you if you want to talk. As an interested observer, not another copper.'

He sighed. 'We're usually so efficient, spot on with where to go next, but half an hour or so before Lucie was killed, everybody left for somebody else's home, or at least that's how it felt. We only have the post-mortem report because Stewart started work on Boxing Day so we could have the results as quickly as possible, but then it seemed to come to a dead stop. And I'm not being facetious with that, and then we lost Philip Barker.'

She took hold of his hand. 'You didn't have to investigate that, it was a suicide, so you said.'

'Yes, it was, but he was our victim's father, so the obvious link was there. We had to investigate him anyway. We know he raped Lucie, and we can't trust Lucie's mother. It's such a strange situation. We feel she's only telling us a restricted version of everything, almost as if she doesn't want to find out who killed Lucie.'

'Maybe she believes the vicar did it. You told me at the beginning that she knew your vicar when you took him with you to do the notification of death visit.'

Adam stared at Elise. 'Twenty-odd years ago they were boyfriend and girlfriend. She finished it, not him, because she was too scared to accept the church as a viable concept for the two of them. Well, certainly not for her, yet he couldn't conceive of a life without the church. She was right to do that, it would have been a miserable life for somebody who didn't love God, but he's not said how he felt about losing her. He seems very happy now with Jenna, who's starting to speak like a Yorkshire lass with an American twang.'

Elise smiled. 'You're telling me how you feel about everyone except Steve Rainforth. Is that his name? See, you don't even speak his name that often! Some of the mums at school go to that church, they speak very highly of him and he's wonderful with the kids. Jenna runs a weekly creche, mums and toddlers up to school age, and there's a small play area in the church that's supervised for the children who accompany their parents to the service.'

'And they can't have children of their own,' he said quietly. 'Now I know them both, I can see that would be a disaster. They start IVF soon, so I should imagine they're both sending all their prayers up to their Lord as often as they can.'

'I'm so sorry they can't conceive naturally, but great strides have been made in IVF, and I'm sure they'll be fine. How on earth did we manage to get two at one go without even trying?'

'I have absolutely no idea, I'm sure I wasn't even there that night.'

'And they definitely don't look like mini-Adams at all,' she said with a grin. 'I get so fed up with hearing oh, aren't they alike and don't they look like their dad!'

'I bet Steve would love to hear that,' he mused. 'I might have to pop along to one of his services, just to observe.'

'Well,' Elise said, 'tomorrow is Sunday, the service starts 10.30am.'

CHAPTER TWENTY-FIVE

Adam shared a pew with a somewhat disgruntled Roger Carson. The elderly man stared at him, gave a nod and said, "'ow do.'

'I'm good thanks, you?'

'Yeah, good. You that copper?'

'Yes, never been here before, not for a service anyway. Thought I'd give it a go, I like Reverend Rainforth.'

'Aye, we all do. Speaks a good sermon.'

And that was it. Subject finished for ten minutes.

'You caught him yet?'

Adam turned, a little surprised by further conversation from Roger. 'No, not yet.'

'Thought not. Thought we'd have heard about it if you had.'

Roger had been interviewed by Adam's team – what hadn't come across in the report was his grumpiness.

'Do you have anything further to tell us?' Adam spoke politely.

'Don't think so. There's one or two ladies not coming to church till you catch him though.'

The congregation rose as Steve entered. Adam could see Jenna sitting at the organ and he was impressed. He knew Marjorie Wilson normally played, but he hadn't thought about who would do it when the elderly lady wasn't available. It appeared to fall to Jenna.

Adam could tell from Steve's reaction that he had spotted him. He began the service, and his sermon led on to the unexpected death at Christmas. As he drew near to the end, Steve added a bit that clearly hadn't been in the piece he had put together.

'I'd like everybody to welcome a member of our local police, who has been in charge of the investigation from the start, DI Adam France. He's sitting on the back pew, so if you have anything you feel should be passed on, please have a quick word with him. I'm sure he won't mind, despite him not being here in his official capacity but as a newcomer to our congregation. And welcome to anybody who is new here today, thank you for attending.'

Holy Communion was celebrated, and the service was soon over. Jenna had played the organ faultlessly, clearly a talented musician, and Steve announced that tea, coffee and mince pies were being served in the church hall for those who fancied a drink, or just wanted to stay and chat.

On reflection, and to his surprise, Adam had enjoyed the whole thing. He had remained in his seat during Communion, but had joined in with everything else, and found it a most pleasant experience. In the hope that somebody might want to pass on some information, he followed people into the church hall, where he had a cup of tea and a mince pie. Home-made. There's a difference... he tried not to laugh because he knew Elise would be jealous that he'd had a home-made mince pie.

He looked around for Jenna, intent on congratulating her on her musical talents, but Steve said she had returned to the vicarage to see to their meal.

'And will it be Marjorie next week?'

'It will be Marjorie until she decides she's had enough. I hope she's our organist for many more years, but she's nearly eighty and one day she may just think enough is enough.'

'I enjoyed the service,' Adam said. 'I came really to make myself available if anyone wanted to talk. It can't have been easy for anybody, what happened on Christmas morning. I know they have you, but I thought an extra ear...'

'You've already spoken to almost everyone, so I understand.'

'Yes, I think there's only five left, and we're hoping to see them next week. I'm seeing Marjorie tomorrow after our first visit of the day has been ticked off. We've basically taken the weekend off because we're feeling harassed by the lack of people available to see, and I know that sounds absolutely ridiculous, but I never want another major crime to erupt over the Christmas holiday season.'

'It is a hectic time, but for the church I think we find Easter more in your face. There's lots of services during Holy Week between Palm Sunday and Easter Day, whereas the services are different at Christmas, but still only once a week, with the addition of Midnight Mass. So the populace disappearing is actually not the church's fault, it's more a family gathering issue when people become inaccessible.' He gave a slight laugh. 'It will all be over tomorrow, Adam, and you'll be overrun with people wanting to talk to you.'

It was Adam's turn to laugh. 'Now you're frightening me. I'll have to pass everyone on to Debra. Although if they all have as much to say as Roger Carson did today, they will be very short conversations.'

'You sat on his pew. That was very brave of you. That's two

171

of you that's done that, you and Lucie, and he'll be going into a decline if it continues. Did he glare at you?'

'He did, but we spoke. Not a lot, but he seems convinced it was a man who killed Lucie.'

'And you? Do you have any such feelings?'

'It could be either. It was one slash with a sharp knife. Doesn't take a man's brute strength to do that. It also didn't need to be a big knife, just a sharp one. Either sex could easily have done it, I just think Roger was being a gentleman and not believing a woman could have done it. He does seem to be a bit old school. Could he have done it, Steve?'

'Well, let's look at it carefully. He was first out of the church alongside Lucie. He said happy Christmas to Jenna and I, and shook our hands, then he said happy Christmas to Lucie, before heading off down the path, leaning carefully on his stick which he has to use. He walks slowly, but he does keep active. I kept half an eye on him as he walked down towards the gate because our church path isn't the smoothest, and I know he has to be really careful. Just as an aside, we're having it re-laid this summer, much to the relief of everybody.' He paused.

'As a result, because I daren't take my eyes off Roger, I completely missed seeing what happened to Lucie. I have no idea where she went, and I also didn't think about it. It was a well-attended Midnight Mass – they always are – and I was so busy wishing everybody well. I was really looking forward to a last hot chocolate with Jenna, so I finished my night off with a prayer in the church and then came out to complete locking everything up.'

'And yet you had no idea she was anywhere near? I wonder what she wanted. Did she speak to you at all?'

'Only to respond with amen to her blessing, and she wished both of us a happy Christmas. She seemed a lovely woman, it's an absolute tragedy and has given me sleepless nights, as I'm sure you realise.'

Adam's mind went back to Friday, to the visit he and Debs had made to the churchyard. He needed to watch Steve's face for the next question. 'Do you think Lucie could have been hanging around the churchyard to speak with you?'

Steve frowned. 'But why? I didn't know her. Couldn't even use her name for the blessing because I'd never seen her before. A lot of our little ones who aren't old enough to be confirmed have a blessing, but I always use their Christian name. I couldn't do that without looking a bit stupid and saying what's your name before placing my hand on her head. I've wondered if I should have done just that, but I didn't. I truly had never seen her before, and if she was waiting to speak to me, what on earth could it have been about? It was hardly the right time and place to talk about joining our church, although she would have been very welcome, but it was in the first hour of Christmas Day.'

Adam nodded. 'I'm not saying anything you did was wrong, we're struggling to find a reason for Lucie being anywhere near Emily Rowbotham's grave. Was it a specific grave she chose because she knew it? We're arranging to have it professionally cleaned by the way, there are blood stains on it.'

Steve looked troubled. 'But it's one of the older graves. I've never seen any flowers on it, so presumably Emily has no family left after all this time. And Lucie couldn't have been using it to hide behind, it's not big enough. There are plenty of really large gravestones that our little ones race around and hide behind, but that one's quite small. When I found Lucie, her body was virtually covering the actual headstone, and she was only a slightly built woman.'

Adam smiled. 'I'm sorry, I've taken you away from your parishioners, and we're no closer to making any sense of it, are we? Go back and cherish your flock, Steve. Thank you for the service, I enjoyed it, much to my surprise. I can't remember the last time I prayed, but today I did for Debra's husband, who's really not well at all.'

'I'm sorry to hear that. Please pass on my best wishes to both of them. And thank you for putting in an appearance, Adam, I think our people will feel comforted by it, and know you're not ignoring anything.'

They shook hands and Adam walked down the path, veering off to go to Emily Rowbotham's grave. The stone had been cleaned of years of grime and the name now glowed with an almost translucent light. The blood had disappeared, and there was a bunch of small chrysanthemums laid across the body of the grave. He stood for a moment taking it in, but somehow knew there was nothing strange going on. A member of this church had done the right thing by this grave, and knowing forensics had returned the church to Steve and seeing the crime scene tape removed, had cleaned it up. Adam hoped Emily was looking down and appreciating it. He lightly touched the headstone, and said, 'Sleep tight, Emily.'

There was no one at home when Adam got there, so he had a quick shower and changed into joggers and sweatshirt. Now he felt truly comfortable, but wondered where his family was. He checked if there was a match on television, saw there was so he put it on. Church and football, what could be more right for a Sunday!

Just as the match was starting, the boys came tearing through the back door and hurtled around looking for him. He tried to hide, but couldn't hold in his laughter.

'Found him,' Alfie called, and William appeared a few seconds later.

'You not got a mother?' he asked.

'Nope, not here.'

'Not here? Where is she?'

'Helping old Mrs Jackson carry her big Christmas tree to the grass verge because the council are collecting them tomorrow.'

Adam looked out of the window, and sure enough Elise was across the road, a huge tree now decorating the verge. She had clearly already completed the job, and was chatting with the old lady. He wasn't required as backup muscle, and he knew Elise wouldn't have asked anyway.

'Anybody want a hot chocolate? And where have you been? You're scruffy!'

'Yes please, Dad.' Both boys spoke at once, so he pulled out four hot chocolate pods, checked the water level in the machine, and began to make the drinks, leaving Elise's until she arrived home.

'We've been to the park.' William started to explain their mucky state. 'It was a bit muddy on the football pitch, but it's been brilliant. Will you go with us next weekend, Dad?'

He looked at the state of them and groaned. 'Of course I will, lads,' he said.

CHAPTER TWENTY-SIX

The briefing room was busy from about seven. The little coffee machine and the battered electric kettle were working overtime as everybody came in frozen; hot drinks were a priority before they had to go back outside and brave it all again.

'I really hate Mondays,' Vicky confessed. 'It's always noisy because no one knows what they're doing and everybody's in to find out their jobs.'

'I really hate Mondays just because they're Mondays,' one of the uniforms grumbled. 'If Monday was Friday, it would all be a lot better.' Nobody had an answer to that, and they all turned as Adam walked through the door.

He looked around, his eyes wide. 'Couldn't you lot sleep? It is Monday, you know, and this could be a long week because I want a murderer locked up by the end of it.'

'If we manage that by the end of today,' Debra said, 'does that mean we get the rest of the week off?'

'Just get me a cup of the delicious coffee, wench, and let's crack on with things. How's Dave?'

'Recovering. I think that's the best way of describing it.

Kara's back home now so the place is a bit livelier. And thank you for the flowers, boss. That was a lovely thought and much appreciated.'

'You're very welcome. We'll have a quick briefing this morning, get the foot soldiers out and about doing what foot soldiers do, and we can get off to this building company. I made the mistake of telling Elise about it, so now I'm on a mission to get a brochure from them. She's fancying having some bespoke work done in our bedroom, so this case looks like it's going to cost me a lot of money. And what's worse, we've had to buy new shoes for the kids that cost nearly as much as buying a new house.'

'You turning into Scrooge?'

'I fear so,' he admitted, and he picked up his coffee to go and get his lads and lasses sorted for their Monday 'first day back after the holidays' work.

Barkers Bespoke Building Ltd. was a very attractive-looking company. The front of the building had obviously been made by the business themselves, and it stood out like a beacon amongst the metal and glass of other companies on the business park.

They exited the car and walked up to the main door. Debra stroked it. 'This is magnificent,' she whispered.

'You don't have to whisper,' Adam said. 'I'm sure they can't hear you, and I'm just as sure that if they could they'd be chuffed by what you said. Come on, let's see what they have to say about their ex-boss.'

They opened the door and it seemed to glide. A buzzer sounded and a young woman appeared instantly from a small office at the back of the room. She stood behind the reception desk and smiled at them.

'Can I help you?'

'DI Adam France and DS Debra Jessop. We'd like a few minutes with Mr Lucas, please.' Both officers held up their warrant cards.

The girl didn't look fazed. 'Can I ask you to take a seat,' she said, pointing to a seating area to her right. 'Mr Lucas always enters via our back door and I haven't actually seen him this morning. I'll go and check that he's in before I send you through to an empty office.'

Adam and Debra did as instructed, and Debra sighed as she sank into the chair. 'These are lovely, comfier than my lounge furniture.'

The girl was away about a minute, and returned with the welcome news that Mr Lucas was in and she would take them through to him.

James Lucas was tall, dressed in jeans and a sweatshirt bearing the company logo. He shook their hands, and they sat on the two chairs facing his desk. 'I've asked Maxie to bring in some tea and coffee. I've never had a visit from the police before. I've no idea why you're here but I'm absolutely certain you could use a hot drink on this freezing day.'

Adam smiled. He liked this man. 'Thank you, sir, it will be appreciated. As this is a private and possibly personal matter, we won't speak of it until your receptionist has delivered the drinks.'

'That's fine. Please excuse my casual appearance, I normally wear a suit, make myself look a bit more like the boss, but today I have two new starters. Seventeen-year-old lads who know nothing at the moment but will by the end of the day. When I become the company trainer, a suit isn't appropriate. Jeans and a sweatshirt are. By tomorrow both new starters will be wearing our sweatshirts and they'll know how to use a handsaw as well as a power saw.'

Adam looked around the office. 'I'm impressed. I assume

you've fitted everything out all the way through? The outside looks pretty good as well.'

'I put my smartest workers on to do it. I bought the business from a friend, and in five years we've doubled the size of the workforce and doubled the turnover.'

There was a knock on the door, and it opened smoothly. Maxie pushed in a small trolley on wheels that held tea and coffee pots, and cups and saucers, along with milk and sugar. There was also a plate of biscuits.

'Thank you, Maxie,' James Lucas said. 'Can you make sure we're not disturbed until our visitors have left the property, please? And can you tell Richard and Jonathan, the two new lads, I've been delayed, but I'll be with them shortly?'

Maxie said she would, and she disappeared quietly. It seemed it was a very quiet business, considering joiners used hammers and saws that were all noisy implements.

They waited until they had drinks in front of them before Adam spoke. 'Mr Lucas, we're here about a man called Philip Barker.'

Lucas nodded before asking them to call him James. 'Please, continue,' he added.

'Philip Barker died last week, and we're learning things about him. This is really just a loose ends kind of visit, because we've been led to understand that this business was started by Mr Barker.'

'It was, and I owe Philip everything. I was told over the weekend that he had died and I'm truly sorry. I had huge respect for him, for his skills, his man management. As you've probably realised he had a problem with drink, and it cost him everything. I was very lucky to have an understanding bank manager who backed me when I wanted to buy the business from Philip, and I'm happy to say the bank manager has never regretted that decision.'

He hesitated for a moment. 'Philip saw the influx of funds from my purchase of the business as another money pot to buy drink. I know eventually he was thrown out by Angela, but I haven't seen him for years. He taught me everything I know. His work was exquisite. If you've seen where he lived with Angela, you'll know. I vowed I would work to that same standard when I took on the massive bank loan, and that has now been cleared and we couldn't be in a better position. But I have to stress, we wouldn't be having this conversation if Philip hadn't succumbed to alcoholism.' He picked up his cup of tea. 'There are still five workers here from the Philip Barker days – they were the ones that persuaded me to keep the name, stressing how good a reputation the business had.'

'Your wood is sourced from sustainable forests?' Debra asked.

'It is. It should be the way everyone works. Our prices reflect that, we aren't cheap fly by nights, but I believe that if you want a good, last for ever type of job you need the finest wood and the finest craftsmen. Neither of those come cheap. All that I'm saying to you will be said to those new apprentices I'll be working with very shortly.'

'We understand you had the role of foreman for Philip?'

'I did and had so much respect for him. And I would still be foreman if it wasn't for the damn drink.'

Adam saw the sudden anger flash across his face, and knew it was because James was all too aware of what had been lost due to Philip's drink problem. 'When did you last see Philip Barker?'

'The day we officially signed over the business to me, 21st August 2021. I'd been running everything on my own for months, so apart from me transferring a lot of money to him, nothing really changed. The main change was the lads stopped calling me James and started calling me boss. That took more getting used to than the knowledge that I now owned my own company and was doing the job I had trained most of my life to do.'

Debra finished her drink and placed the cup and saucer on the tray. 'I might just say we don't get cups and saucers back at the station,' she said with a smile.

'We treat everyone the same. It doesn't matter if they're buying an entire bedroom suite costing thousands of pounds or just popping in to organise getting a quote, every customer is a cup-and-saucer customer. And we now seem to include police officers in that as well!'

'Do you have a brochure? I'm under instructions from my dearly beloved to bring something back with me,' said Adam. 'She's after having a complete built-in suite of furniture in our bedroom. I may be needing a bank manager as friendly as yours was.'

James slid open his side drawer and took out two brochures. He handed one to each of them. 'The handwritten number on the back is my personal number. Call that if ever you want to open a discussion. Some jobs are personal, some are done by my staff. Is there anything else you need to know?'

Both officers stood. 'I don't think so, James. Thank you for your co-operation, it's been a pleasure to sit just for a few minutes in this little haven of timber,' Adam said. He reached across to shake his hand, and Debra followed on with the same action.

'I'll walk out with you, then I'm off to get to know my new lads. If you need anything further, you have my personal mobile.'

Adam turned as they reached the door. 'How much do you know of the relationship between Angela and Philip?'

'Precious little. Angela said they were splitting up because of the alcohol problem, so I didn't ask any more. Everything has been the alcohol problem in his life.' They thanked him once again, turned to wave as they reached their vehicle, but he had disappeared back into the warmth.

They sat in the car, once again shivering. 'Nice feller,' Debra said.

'He is, very polite. And obviously still in touch with Angela Barker.'

She frowned as she looked at him.

'They're no longer in any sort of business together, yet he knew Philip was dead, and he didn't ask how he died, which leads me to think he already knows. I think Angela got straight onto him as soon as she knew about it.'

'You think it's a bit... sinister?'

'Not really. They were the closest of friends until Philip was out of the business, I just felt it was strange that he didn't ask questions. And if he didn't ask questions, it's because he knew the answers.'

Debra switched on the engine, moved the gear stick into drive, then kept her foot on the brake. 'That's why you're a DI and I'm a DS. My mind's not as twisted as yours.' The car surged forward as she lifted her right foot, and headed back to the station. She'd loved having a cup and saucer, perhaps it was time to start educating her fellow coppers.

'Why didn't you ask him if we could see the workshops?' she asked.

'Thought you'd be bored,' he responded. 'You know, being a mere little woman.'

'You're on such dodgy ground you're in danger of sinking and never being found again.'

'Well,' he said, trying not to smile, 'I bought you some beautiful flowers on Saturday, and all you're doing is getting violent with me. Shame on you, DS Jessop!'

CHAPTER TWENTY-SEVEN

dam took the decision to avoid a return to the station. While they were out they would call round to see if Marjorie the organist was available. He hoped she was home from her Christmas break with her family, but he knew there were no guarantees.

The elderly lady was actually outside in her front garden when they pulled up beside her cottage.

'Hello,' she said as they walked up her path. 'You're my police visitors?'

'We are,' Adam responded. 'DI Adam France and DS Debra Jessop.' Once again they produced their warrant cards, but she didn't even check them.

'Cataracts,' she explained. 'Having them done in a couple of weeks, but for now I just don't bother trying to read anything. Come inside, it's far too cold out here.'

The heat in the cottage was stifling, but nobody complained.

'Can I get you two a drink?'

'No thank you, Mrs Wilson. We've just had one. We want to ask you a couple of questions about Christmas Eve, then we can leave you to whatever you were doing outside. I need to record our chat so I can type up your statement accurately. Is that okay?' Debra asked.

'Of course. You do what you have to do. I was only checking if any plants needed some protection in this bitter cold. We really could do with a couple of warmer days. It was even colder on Christmas Eve. I walked down to the church for Mass, even though Steve offered to collect me, but I love Christmas and thought a walk would make everything so much more festive.' She laughed. 'By the time I sat at the organ I could hardly feel my fingers. I managed to warm them through before I had to play, but didn't manage a little practice session first.'

Debra smiled at the old lady. 'How do you read the music if you can't see?'

'I don't is the simple answer. I get away with it at Christmas because carols are carols, and I've been playing them for about seventy years. I know the music, play them by ear. It's when we introduce new hymns that I struggle, but Steve's been very good about it and stuck to all the old stuff for the past few months. And of course we can always call on Jenna if there's a real problem.'

Adam nodded. 'It was Jenna on the organ for yesterday's service.'

'You went?'

'I did. Thoroughly enjoyed it. I wanted to make myself available to people in case they had anything to pass on to the police, but nobody did. I had quite a chat with Steve, but he's very easy to talk to.'

'Oh, he is. He's built this congregation from about three regulars a week to what you saw on Sunday. He's a proper community vicar, puts kids first which is no bad thing.'

'So, can we take you back to Christmas Eve? As you know, we're investigating the murder of a twenty-four-year-old woman called Lucie Barker, who was killed in the churchyard. We've spoken to almost every member of the congregation from that night with absolutely zero information coming from it. Our investigators are out today to clear these last few up, one of which is you. You've had a good Christmas with your family?'

'It's been wonderful. I've been so spoilt. I stayed at my daughter's, but also had a couple of nights with my grandson and his partner and their new baby. I've loved every minute, but I'm glad to be back home in my own little place where I can blast the heating out if I'm cold, or turn it off when I start to feel guilty at the money I'm squandering.' She laughed as she said the last bit.

'Don't feel guilty,' Debra said. 'At your age it's important to stay warm, so if you feel cold, crank it up. No guilt!'

'That is what Steve says about the church. About two years ago we'd managed to raise enough money to instal new heating, and it made such a difference. Now it always feels warm and it's a pleasure to walk into it. I turned the heating off in here when I walked down to the church on Christmas Eve, knowing my son-in-law, who had earlier collected my suitcase and all my gifts for the family, was making a second trip to pick me up after my organ stint at Midnight Mass. I figured it was a bit extravagant leaving the heating on for over a week when I wasn't even here.'

'Just a bit,' Adam agreed. 'So you walked down the lane outside your home. It's not too far to the church, is it?'

'No, it's why I started going to that church many years ago. My husband and I bought this place soon after we were married. It's worth quite a bit more now than we paid for it then, but I've loved living so close to the place I feel most at home in. The church is my refuge. Just as it is for Steve. I've found that if I need Steve for anything, it's advisable to check the church first. He had set it up, got it toasty warm and put all the service sheets out on the pews well before anyone got there.'

'What time did you arrive?'

'I checked my watch as I passed by the vicarage because somebody was knocking on the door. It was 11.20, which I was quite pleased about because it meant I could have a few minutes of prayer before I had to sit at the organ.'

'Can we take a step back?' Adam asked. 'Somebody was at the vicarage door?'

'Yes. I thought it was a bit silly, because Steve and Jenna would have been in the church, but actually only Steve must have been in doing the set-up. Jenna answered the door at the vicarage. I could see her talking to the person, and got the impression there was some sort of upset or disagreement, but please don't take that as being correct. It was only a visual impression and I have cataracts,' she said with a laugh. 'Jenna could simply have been telling her how to get round to the church door without falling over gravestones. You probably know there's a direct path from the vicarage that goes across the churchyard and to the front door.'

'Did you recognise the person?'

'Not then. That was later when the congregation started to come in. I was playing a very quiet and peaceful "Silent Night", something that I don't have to think about, and one or two in the congregation began to sing along to it. It was a very spontaneous act and I was loving it.'

Debra smiled. 'I wish I'd been here. It sounds perfect.'

'Oh it was. It's the first time I've ever experienced spontaneous singing to church music being played in the background, and it was so special. Something I'll never forget. I couldn't stop talking about it when my son-in-law collected me.'

'And the person you later recognised?' Adam drew them back into what he really wanted to know.

'It was that young lady. When I saw her at the door of the vicarage she was standing under the light of the lamp above their door. I didn't know her, obviously, but she had a light-coloured winter jacket on, a puffa type. That jacket walked into the church a few seconds before the service started, and she sat on the back pew. It made me smile because I could imagine what Roger Carson was thinking.'

Adam couldn't help but picture that jacket covered in blood, lying on a grave.

'Everything went smoothly throughout the service, it was so lovely. And I knew we still had verse four of "O Come all ye Faithful" to come, which always raises the roof with the volume of the singing. It's a very special moment singing that verse, which is only ever sung on Christmas morning.'

'And Holy Communion was celebrated?' Majorie could certainly talk, but she seemed to have excellent recall of that night, Adam thought.

'Yes, everyone participated, and the young lady had a blessing. In view of what happened later, I hope she felt the power of that blessing, because it is such a special feeling.'

'And at the end?'

'I was one of the first to leave because I knew a car was waiting for me. I followed Roger and the young lady out, but I didn't notice where either of them went because I was rushing to get down the path and to the car. Does any of this help? And are you sure you don't want a hot drink?'

Debra smiled at Marjorie. 'You're so lovely, but no, we'll be searching out toilets all morning if we have any more drinks. It's a hazard of the job. Thank you for all of this information. I'll pop back hopefully tomorrow with your statement for you to read through and sign, but if it's difficult I can read it to you. Is that okay?'

'Of course. I'm sorry I've rabbited on, once I start I have trouble stopping.'

Adam smiled at her. 'I've enjoyed every minute of this,

ANITA WALLER

you're a pleasure to interview, and we didn't have to use the handcuffs and taser!'

'I'm relieved about that. It would be difficult playing the organ, or even my own piano, in handcuffs.'

She walked with them to the door, and waved as they drove away.

They picked up two lattes from the Costa drive-through and took them back to the station. Neither spoke until they were in Adam's office.

'This is the first new piece of information we've had since day one. Why did Lucie Barker go to the vicarage before the church? What the hell don't we know that we should be aware of? Obviously Jenna must have thought it wasn't worth mentioning, so are we to assume she was merely asking how to get to the main door, or what time the service started, or could she go in then or did she have to wait? Behind all of this we have a newcomer to the church who didn't know the system, especially of an annual service. Why has this not cropped up before now?'

'Maybe there's only Jenna who knew what Lucie did. If she just wanted information about start times, as you've suggested, it wouldn't be worth mentioning. Maybe Jenna simply forgot about the young woman at her door. I know it's new information but we do know she arrived safely at the church. The attack happened later when the service was over.'

Adam took off his jacket and sat at his desk. 'Sit down, we need to think and talk this through. And I want to listen to everything that Marjorie said, just in case we missed anything.' He sipped at his coffee. 'Ouch, that's bloody hot.'

'It's coffee, boss. It's meant to be hot. We bought it to warm us up.'

'Oh shut up, smart arse. You sound like my wife when I've made some daft statement.'

'In your defence,' Debra grinned, 'it is bloody hot. Take the lid off, don't drink it through the little hole.'

'So what's our next move? Speak to Jenna? Let's see what she remembers of her visitor. She may not remember much, because nobody knew Lucie, and they were about to start Midnight Mass, which is stressful enough without having strangers knocking at your door.'

'Is that tomorrow's plan? Or do you think it's so urgent we need to go back to where we've just left and speak to Jenna right now?'

'Are you being a smart arse again?'

CHAPTER TWENTY-EIGHT

And Tuesday morning brought sunshine. It made the world feel like a better place, even though it was still cold. Reports from all members of the congregation had now been completed and uploaded to the file, with only one person saying they had noticed the young woman but hadn't seen her after the service had finished.

Marjorie appeared to be the only one who had observed anything, and that had simply been seeing Lucie at the vicarage door, which didn't particularly help because that sighting had been prior to the service and not after. Lucie had definitely been alive immediately after the service, the last official sighting being when she said happy Christmas on leaving the church.

'Let's go ask Jenna if Lucie had anything to say when she knocked on her door. I must admit, if there had been anything significant, like somebody is following me, can you help me, I'd hope Jenna might have thought to mention it.' Adam looked at his watch. 'It's a bit early to go, we'll hang on an hour.'

'I agree, I think Jenna would have said something when we first spoke with them if it held any significance. We're clutching at straws because this is the first new bit of information we've had for days and days.' Debra paused for a moment. 'I think we should harass Angela a bit more. We both feel she's holding something back, and that something may just be the missing link in all of this.'

'Right, here's a plan. Let's drop in on Angela, maybe go out to Chesterfield and take a look at Philip Barker's place now we have access to his keys after forensics have closed down the case, then come back to Sheffield to see Jenna.'

They began their plan in Chesterfield, entering the small terraced house with a degree of trepidation. Debra always felt uncomfortable entering someone's home when it was empty, and this one felt truly empty.

It was very clear that Philip hadn't used any of his immense skills to make this a home that was the equivalent of the one he had left. It felt as if it was unloved; it held the bare minimum of furniture, with only a coffee table and one armchair facing a small television perched on a wooden box. Debra guessed the carpet and curtains had been sold along with the house, and were of reasonable quality, but she knew she wouldn't want to sit in that room for any length of time. It was unloved and unwelcoming.

There were no drawers to check through, although several empty lager tins were on the mantelpiece above an old electric fire. She wandered around the room, but soon left it. It told her nothing except Philip Barker hadn't only walked away from his marriage, he'd walked away from the other thing he loved in life: joinery.

Adam had taken on the kitchen. He was working his way through the cupboards, but it was clear there was nothing to find.

'I'll start upstairs,' she said. 'It's so sad that he didn't do any joinery in his home. This is nothing like the house he shared with Angela, is it?'

'Nothing at all. This is really just somewhere he came home to at night to sleep off the beer. It's so sad. A quick look upstairs and we're done.'

'I'll make a start in his bedroom.' Debra climbed the stairs but stopped halfway up. She was wrong, he had done some work and it was beautiful. The banister had been replaced, along with the spindles and the base plate. It was beautiful to hold, and so smooth she knew he had to have been sober to have created such exquisite workmanship.

'Adam,' she called, 'come and look at this!'

Adam joined her and she showed him the banister.

'My God. He could do something like this as an alcoholic? This is stunning. Such a huge talent, and he took his own life.' Just as Debra had done, he ran his hands down the banister. 'This feels amazing, so tactile. What a skill to have.'

Debra was sitting on the stairs, just looking at it. 'No wonder he ran such a successful business. And to pass those skills on to his employees is something else. This sort of stuff comes from more than just a love of woodwork, it's an absolute affinity with the raw product, isn't it? My dad loves wood. He's got a shed, but he didn't go out and buy one, he went and bought the wood and built it to his own specs. And he loves to whittle. Mum has little wooden mushrooms dotted all over the garden, which she loves, and she never knows when he's making one, it just appears. But he's nowhere near this level.' She sighed deeply. 'Such a waste that he's gone.'

They both sat for a moment, lost in admiration. 'You know,' Debs said thoughtfully, 'I think that's possibly why there's only the minimum of stuff in the lounge. There was literally nothing for me to check in there, but if he had plans in his head, he wouldn't want to be buying stuff until they began to happen. I know there was the awful accusation of rape hanging over his memory, but this wasn't the thing to do, was it? To take his own life. He was still quite a young man, with nothing wrong with him except a love of alcohol.'

Adam stood. 'Let's get on with it, this is too depressing. I'll finish off in the kitchen, then take the bathroom. Are there only two bedrooms?'

'I don't know, I've not got beyond here. This beautiful work stopped me in my tracks. I'll make a start in the main bedroom now.'

She continued up, running her hand along the banister all the way. *Sometimes*, she thought, *it's a pleasure to climb stairs.* And deep in her heart she knew Philip would have felt like that.

The bedroom was disastrous, with a horrible smell of faeces, alcohol, and death itself. She stood in the doorway for a minute, just taking in the scene. It was a mess, with the bedding half on the floor and half on the bed. Empty vodka and whisky bottles were numerous, as were empty and full cans of beer and lager.

There was a small television on the bedside table that had a huge crack across it, and it was just a table, no drawers to keep anything in for her to check. Three of the four pillows were still on the bed so she lifted them to no avail; there was a pen, and Debra guessed he'd scrawled his final note with it.

There were no drinking vessels of any description, so she had to assume he'd drunk straight from the bottle or can. The tablets he had imbibed and left scattered around had all been removed, along with their packaging, by the forensics team. Everything was listed on their report and she knew Adam would attach theirs to it. Adam's would say very little as there wasn't much to see.

The small wardrobe held a couple of T-shirts and a pair of

jeans. A plastic box in the bottom held underpants and socks. This man lived life pared down to the very minimum.

She closed the door gently behind her and moved to the second bedroom. He had woodworking tools. She took out her phone and began to take photographs. She couldn't put a name to many of them, but they were clean, laid out on a small collapsible table, and none of them were power tools. This man had been of the old school, a woodworking genius. This was clearly his work room where he had fashioned all those identical spindles, lovingly carved by hand, probably with a can of beer by his side. Debra knew that when she returned back downstairs, she would be unable to resist stroking the header of the newel post. She needed to see what he had created at the bottom, to enhance his small hallway.

This room was tidy. It was nothing like the chaos of his bedroom where he slept. He was proud of this space, proud of his tools. It was a room in which he spent more time than any other, except maybe the public bar of the Brown Bear. She wanted to stamp her feet very loudly and scream what a waste of a life, but her professionalism won through and she took it all in without disturbing too much. It wasn't necessary. This room was Philip Barker. And Philip Barker appeared to be two different people.

She could hear Adam in the bathroom, so she went downstairs, sliding her hand gently down the banister. The header of the newel post was an acorn about nine inches tall, with oak leaves gently nestling the nut in their veins. Tears touched her eyes. There was love in that acorn, and she hoped that whoever bought this house when it was put on the market would appreciate what Philip Barker had created.

They had found nothing to help with the investigation, but Debra's impression of the man had shifted. They could now sign him off as case concluded, but she would never forget how she had felt seeing what he had created on those stairs. And she would appreciate Angela's home even more now, because that house was filled with Philip's work.

She watched Adam descend the stairs, and simply pointed to the acorn as he reached the bottom.

'My God,' he said. 'I'd want to buy this property for that alone.' His hand involuntarily moved towards it, and he stroked it.

'The second bedroom holds his tools,' she said. 'No power tools, all hand tools. I think the reason the house isn't particularly cosy isn't just down to alcoholism, I suspect there was an issue on the stairs, maybe missing spindles, or the banister was broken. I think he spent time doing this because it was the urgent bit, and I tell you what, I would have loved to see how he finished off the rest of the house.'

'And he trained James Lucas.' Adam groaned. 'I feel a severe drain on our finances coming on, because when my Elise sees that brochure, she's going to be picking out her wardrobes in the first two minutes.'

Debra couldn't resist a last caress of the acorn before they locked the door behind them and headed back to the car.

Adam took the wheel, and Debra sank back and closed her eyes. 'What an amazing morning. And I was dreading it. It just shows how we judge people, doesn't it? I feel as though the Philip Barker we've heard so much bad stuff about isn't the same person we've come across today. I allowed myself a bit of prejudging when I started in the lounge because it was so spartan, but now I understand. And I don't think I'm wrong.'

'I feel a little overwhelmed. By an acorn! I need to go home, find a sharp knife and whittle. I once went to the Louvre, saw the *Mona Lisa* through tears, and wanted to come home and paint a copy. I think beauty strikes a lot of people like that, and it usually takes us by surprise. It certainly did me, and I'll never forget the things that made me feel that way.'

She turned her head to look at him. 'Through tears? You saw the *Mona Lisa* through tears?'

He nodded. 'I did. And if you ever go to the Louvre, you'll know exactly why.'

CHAPTER TWENTY-NINE

They tossed a coin to decide whether to see Jenna first or Angela.

Jenna won on the basis that she would be an easy one because she wasn't really involved in anything, and they only needed a couple of minutes with her simply to confirm Marjorie's story.

'You got Marjorie's statement on you?'

Debra patted her bag. 'Thought I could nip in while we were here and get her signature, then that's something else crossed off. For a case that's at a standstill, my to-do list is mighty long.'

'Did you type it up?'

'I did. I actually wanted to listen to it again, so I typed it up while I was doing that. She was so lovely, and so interesting. Another talented person. It's been that sort of a case, hasn't it? Even the victim was super talented, with her own craft business. You think Angela will take that on?'

'Unless she's a fast learner I don't see how she can. On your to-do list have you got a spot to fit in a telephone chat with the two ladies who worked part time for Lucie? Maybe we need their take on things. If the telephone chat reveals anything that requires something deeper, we can go and see them, but they're not really involved so I'm hesitant to make it an official statement taking job.'

Debra sighed. 'I'll add it to my list.' She took out her phone, pulled up her notes app and added the two craft ladies to the list.

Adam pulled up outside the vicarage. They walked up the path. It was still bitterly cold, but with the sun out it made things seem vaguely springlike. There were a few primulas dotted around that were trying their best to appear as though the sun meant it was time to flower, and Debra fervently hoped they were right.

She knocked on the door and Steve answered. 'Five more minutes and you'd have had to track me down in the church,' he said. 'Sometimes I write my sermon here but if I'm not sure where it's going, I write it in the vestry. It helps.'

'We won't keep you. Actually it's Jenna we want a quick word with, then we'll leave you alone because we're going over to see Lucie Barker's mother.'

'Is Angela okay?'

'You still haven't spoken with her?' Adam asked.

'No. It's difficult...'

'She's in your church catchment area, isn't she? Maybe you should contact her in your official capacity, although I'm not sure she gives Christianity much credence. She didn't do the Midnight Mass with Lucie, did she?'

'No, and you're right of course. I should contact her.'

'Do you have, or need, her number?'

'No, she said it out loud to you that first night. It's now in my nuisance of a memory for ever.'

'You kidding me?'

Steve laughed. 'No, I'm not. I've got this strange thing

where my memory can't forget numbers, even though I have to keep a diary for appointments and suchlike. But numbers are always there.' He recited Angela's number to prove his point, and Adam took out his phone to check it. He gave a small whistle.

'I'm impressed. We've just been talking about all the different talents the people involved in this case have, but this one really impresses me.'

'It comes in handy. The Bible is numbers. John 1 verse 3. Luke 6 verse 10. It's all numbers. I wish it remembered words and stuff, but it doesn't. So my spelling isn't the best, but my numbers are.'

Debra shook her head. 'Now I'm totally upset. I don't have any talents or skills, can't knit, can't crochet, can't ice cakes and keep them looking like cakes. I'm pretty useless.'

'You solve cases,' Steve pointed out with a laugh, 'and I don't doubt that over the next couple of days, now the world is back to normal, the killer will be apprehended and I'll be having to change my sermon yet again to reflect that. It will be a blessed day when that happens though, so don't let me moaning about having to change my sermon put you off tracking down this killer. Anyway, you want a cuppa?'

'A very quick one,' Adam said, 'just while we're chatting to Jenna. Is she in?'

'She will be very shortly. It's been mums and toddlers morning in church, she'll be putting away the toys right now, so I'll make all of us a drink.'

They followed Steve through to the kitchen, which was beautifully warm. 'Wonderful,' Debra breathed. 'We've had a cold, cold morning and this is heaven.'

'Coffee?' Steve asked, and they both said yes. It was already brewed and within seconds cups were in front of them.

'We went somewhere yesterday where we were offered a

choice of tea or coffee, plus biscuits, and with cups and saucers. And this was a factory, of sorts.' Debra grinned. 'It was wonderful, but I don't think I'll be suggesting it for back at the station, there it seems the bigger the mug the better.'

'We've got a china tea service, it's in a cardboard box down in the cellar,' Steve said. 'Jenna was horrified at the thought of using it because I'd inherited it from my mother. Said we'd break them, so they're now packed away.'

'Well I haven't got one,' Debra said, sipping at her coffee, 'but it's on my list now I've actually drunk from a china cup. And I'm not waiting to inherit my mum's set, because she's going to live for ever, I hope.'

The front door opened and they heard Jenna shout, 'Do we have guests?'

'We do,' Steve answered his wife. 'You want coffee or tea?'

'Coffee if it's done,' she said, entering the kitchen. 'I've only walked from the church and I'm frozen. What's with this weather? It's absolutely freezing out there.'

Adam laughed. 'It's January. Tends to be like this at this time of year.'

Jenna looked at the two detectives. 'You have news for us?'

Adam shook his head. 'Not the sort of news you mean, no news of an arrest but at least we find people at home now when we call on them. We came to see what you can remember about that night.'

'Me? Very little. I was too scared to remember much. We were in a graveyard waiting for someone to come and help us, with a dead body, and we had no knowledge of who had killed her. And it was freezing. That's my main memory. And blood. I tried to help Lucie, but there was so much blood, on her, on the grave, on me, on Steve, and it was all too late.'

'Can I take you back to a little earlier, to before the service? Lucie knocked at the vicarage door and you answered.'

Jenna frowned. Then her face seemed to clear. 'Oh my God, was that Lucie? I thought it was a child, possibly a teenager. I couldn't really see because I was just about to put my contact lenses in when I heard the knock at the door. She was a bit of a blur, I'm afraid. It was Lucie?' she repeated.

'It was. She was seen by Marjorie on her way to take up her position at the organ.'

'I didn't know, whoever it was. They asked what time the service started, was it midnight? I said no, it would be around 11.30, and usually finished around 12.20. I honestly thought it was a young girl. I feel even worse about the whole situation now.'

'No need to,' Adam said. 'No one could possibly have guessed what was to happen later. And that's you crossed off Debra's famous to-do list.'

'I think I pointed to our private path so she could go directly across the churchyard instead of by the road, but that was it. That poor girl, she could have been watched from before she went in to the church, and none of us knew.'

She took her coffee from Steve, sipped at it and sighed. 'As Steve says, that warms the cockles of your heart. I'm not sure what cockles of the heart are, but it's in my list of Yorkshire sayings that I've had to learn since marrying Steve.'

'Thanks for clearing that up about your late-night caller,' Debra said. 'Hopefully we'll have more positive news for you next time we see you.'

The two officers handed their mugs back to Steve, who walked with them down to their car. 'I will contact Angela,' he said to Adam. 'I've been a little cowardly about this, but she has neither ex-husband nor daughter now, and as you pointed out, it's part of my job to shepherd my flock, even when they don't appreciate being part of my flock.'

'Jenna isn't aware you know each other?'

'Not as far as I know. Jenna came into my life as a member of my congregation at the last church I had. That was five years or so ago. We married a couple of years ago, but it would have been sooner if I hadn't been so scared of commitment. And I blame Angela for that. I was wholly committed to her, I loved her, but she couldn't love God, she said. She didn't see herself as a vicar's wife, and she walked away. Jenna did see herself as a vicar's wife, and she stayed. It was a real shock that night when Angela opened the door. I recognised her immediately. When you love somebody as deeply as I had loved her, you will always know them instantly. I just hadn't known of her marriage to Philip Barker. But I will ring her and if she wants to see me, I'll visit her.'

'Good man,' Adam said. 'But maybe you should talk to Jenna about the situation first.'

Steve laughed. 'I think that might be a smart move, Adam. Can I go and write my sermon now?'

Adam and Debra drove off with a wave of their hands, and Debra smiled. 'I like him. Doesn't make out he's more than he is. I've known other vicars over the years who look down their noses at you, but he's not like that. Yep, good bloke.'

They did a quick diversion to Marjorie's cottage, who answered the door rubbing her eyes. 'Sorry I took so long, it was warm and I nodded off. You need me to sign something?'

Adam remained in the car, but gave her a quick wave. Debra followed her inside and handed the statement to her. 'I can't read it because of my eyes, so you'll have to read it to me, then I'll sign it.'

'No problem,' Debra said, and they sat at the kitchen table while Debra read every word to her.

'That's fine,' she said and took the pen held out to her. Debra guided her hand to the signature line, waited until she wrote her name, and then popped the statement back into her bag.

'Thank you, Marjorie,' she said and stood to leave.

'No news yet then,' Marjorie asked.

'No, sorry. But soon.' The old lady waved as they drove away.

'All done. She couldn't see to read it, so I had to read it aloud to her, then get her to sign in the correct place. Hope I never get cataracts. She's just told me at the door that everything she looks at has a yellowish tinge to it.'

'My mum used to say that, and when she had them removed she said it was like living in a different world, so it will be better soon for Marjorie. It's a good job she doesn't need to look at music to play the church organ. It's also a good job she could see enough to know there was somebody at the vicarage door on Christmas Eve.'

Debra looked at her boss. Was there a touch of unease in the way he said those words?

CHAPTER THIRTY

Angela didn't look too thrilled to see them. 'Come in,' she said, grudgingly holding the door open. Debra paid particular attention to the newel post in the hallway. It was topped by a beautiful hand-carved owl. Envy was a word she didn't know much about, but now she did. She couldn't resist touching it as she followed Angela down the hallway.

'I'm assuming you haven't come to give me news about the killer?'

'No, we haven't,' Adam responded tetchily. He was in no mood for a stroppy woman. And he also felt they'd done a full day's work that morning, so if she thought she could get antsy with them, she could think again. He could easily get a key to a cell...

Debra saw a grin briefly flash across his face and wondered what he'd thought about in that split second to cause that reaction. She knew he wasn't too keen on Angela Barker.

'Okay, Angela,' he began. 'It seems to me that out of everybody involved in this case, you're actually the only one without an alibi.'

Debra said nothing. She was wondering where that had come from. They hadn't even covered an alibi for Angela, but he was right, they didn't have one. She must have words with her boss, explain if he was going to bring up stuff like this, she preferred to be forewarned.

Surely... no. He didn't... he couldn't think this woman who had lost her world was the killer they had been seeking since Christmas morning?

She waited to see what would come next. To see if he would need rescuing from a well-aimed kitchen knife, because as a mother of a child who she loved dearly, she wouldn't take that sort of crap from anybody. She held her breath. And watched.

Angela stood and walked to the kitchen sink, leaving the two officers seated at the kitchen table. She turned around holding the glass she had just filled with water.

'You,' she said, pointing at Adam, 'are a singularly stupid man. I no longer have much respect for most men, but when they add stupidity to their DNA the respect disappears altogether.'

Debra drew in her breath and got ready to intervene. But she mostly kept an eye on the stand holding the set of kitchen knives. The complete set of kitchen knives.

Adam smiled. 'Well, Angela, that was the right reaction. If I'd seen panic, if I'd seen fear, any of the reactions shown by guilty people, you might very easily have found yourself in handcuffs, but you got mad with me. Debra sometimes does that, but I should tell you Debra had no idea I was going to say that to you today. Okay, sit down, let's start again.'

Angela brought the glass of water to the table with her, and Debra somehow knew that if Adam said anything else wrong, the glass of water would end up poured over his head. Justifiably so, probably.

'You know,' Angela said, enunciating each word clearly and

carefully, 'that the only thing I had left to live for was my daughter. Our relationship was special; she was my friend, my sister, my confidante, my daughter – and at times when she thought I was being crazy, my mother. I can live without her, I have done for nearly two weeks, but I don't *want* to live without her. And the biggest thing you need to know, DI France, is that I didn't fucking kill her. She's never, in her life, had so much as a smacked hand. We never had to tell her off, chastise her in any way, she was perfect, and somebody out there has killed perfection. But it wasn't me. She was conceived in love and with love, completely, and I believe that was in her genes. If her true father and I had stayed together, she would still be alive, but I couldn't stay with him and I settled for second best, who was also a wonderful man for most of our married life.'

Adam appeared to hold his breath. 'And her true father was Steve Rainforth?'

Angela stared down at her clasped hands. Nobody spoke for a minute and then she lifted her head, stared at the two officers and said, 'Yes.'

She picked up the water and drank from it, then placed it back on the table.

Adam exhaled. 'Thank you for confirming that. Does Steve know?'

'Yes, but he didn't know anything about her until the night she died, when he came with you. As you were leaving I had about thirty seconds to tell him. I'm assuming he got the calculator out when he got home and now believes me. There was never any other man in my life, she was the child of Steve Rainforth. To protect him, me and the baby I let everybody think it was a one-night stand. That wasn't true. By the time Lucie was born, I was Mrs Barker, and she took Philip's surname because we were a family. I never saw Steve again because he finished his training and moved down south to his first church.'

'And you thought you could keep this hidden?' Debra asked.

'Hoped more than thought. It never sat easily with Philip, you know. We wanted another child, but Philip proved to be infertile. It devastated him, and I believe his drinking began to increase little by little from that day onwards.'

'So let me get something very clear. Reverend Rainforth knew nothing about his child until you told him on Christmas morning, after you had been notified of her death?' asked Adam.

'That's right. I would never have told him. And I would never have told Lucie, but a few days before Christmas we'd shared a bottle of wine, and we were talking about people we had loved in our lives, not just partners but family as well, and I mentioned Steve. She knew straight away, so it was confession time. When she found out where he was, she said she wanted to observe from afar before making contact, so would go to his church. I didn't know at that point she meant the Midnight Mass. That's not the ideal time to walk up to a man, a vicar, and say hi, I'm your daughter.'

Adam nodded. 'And she didn't tell him. That's why she was waiting in the churchyard. She wanted him to be the last one out so she could speak with him and only him. Jenna, his wife, had already returned to the vicarage.'

'And despite all this soul searching and secrets being revealed, we're still no closer to finding out who was lurking in that churchyard waiting to kill Lucie.' Debra felt quite disheartened.

'I'm assuming Steve hasn't told us because in some strange way he feels he can't let you down, he's protecting you,' said Adam.

Angela gave a rueful smile. 'That sounds like the Steve I knew. And when I told him he was a father, while standing on my doorstep saying goodbye for the second time in our lives, the shock on his face was evident. It had never crossed his mind that the daughter of mine who had died could possibly be a daughter of his.'

Adam smiled at her. 'It's amazing what a good argument and a bit of hurled criticism can bring out of the woodwork, but thank you for your honesty now, Angela. You have my number if you think of any tiny thing that may help us, but I feel we're getting closer now stuff isn't being withheld. I need to get all of this typed onto a statement form, which will require your signature so one of us will pop back tomorrow with that and we can upload it to our case file.'

'And will it become public knowledge?' Angela asked quietly.

'I hope not, but the next few days will decide that.'

Angela went with them to the door and waited until they had driven away before closing it. Not a word of apology had passed her lips; she wasn't sorry for anything she had said, and she would say it all again if ever it became necessary.

Steve headed for the church, taking a peaceful ten minutes for personal prayer time before entering the vestry for the peace and quiet necessary for writing a sermon. Should he still make reference to the murder, or leave it until they had something concrete to pass on? It was difficult to know what to do, hence the prayer time when he sought guidance. Unfortunately, he didn't get any answers or help; it seemed the Lord was leaving him to his own devices this week.

He poured himself a glass of water, sat at his desk, and opened up his laptop. He stared at the blank screen for what seemed like for ever, and he realised that if he'd been an author and not a vicar, the sight of that blank screen would have created some sort of disastrous feeling deep inside his soul. Which was a bit how he had felt all day.

He'd had a daughter, and he'd lost a daughter.

He shook his head and went back to his sermon.

Jenna had laid claim to the office in the vicarage for the afternoon, on the pretext that it was the new year and she needed to set up a new registration book for the mums and toddlers group. She needed peace, away from church business, and in the warmest room in the place.

But first she had letters to write. Her family in America needed to know how she was, what life was doing to her, when the IVF was starting, and was Steve the Archbishop of Canterbury yet?

Her handwriting was distinctive, sloping to the right. She didn't put dots over the letter i, she drew a tiny flower instead. She liked writing, loved the feel of paper under her hands, loved the idea that in a few days her mum and dad would be reading this, connecting with her. She would enclose one for Sandy and Ben as well, and on each letter she would send all her love.

After she had completed both letters, she put them into one envelope, addressed it to her parents and put an airmail sticker on it. She glanced at the clock. She could nip down to the post office and post it within the hour.

She took another piece of paper, made herself a hot chocolate, and settled back down at the desk. This letter would take much longer, would be much harder to get right, and she had to let the recipient know everything. She sipped at her drink, began to write and didn't stop for over an hour.

She put it into a plain white envelope, sealed it and drew a heart over the pointed end of the flap.

Then she went upstairs, took down her large backpack and put clothes and memories in it. It didn't take long; she didn't have long before Steve was due back. She zipped the backpack up and took it to the cloakroom, hanging it on a hook, before covering it with her jacket.

Ten minutes later her letters to America had gone, and she arrived back at the vicarage at exactly the same time her husband was walking round the corner, returning from his afternoon in church.

She kissed him and they went inside. It was beautifully warm and cosy, and she wanted to cry.

EPILOGUE
WEDNESDAY 8 JANUARY 2025

S teve woke in an empty bed and he smiled. Whoever got up first obeyed the unwritten rule of putting on the coffee machine, and it was usually him. He thought it was strange he couldn't smell coffee, but then realised she may have only been up a minute. He swung his legs out of bed and shivered. No heating on? He glanced at his phone and saw it was only six o'clock. Why was Jenna up? Was she unwell?

He felt a small sense of panic, and hunted around under the bed for his slippers before heading downstairs. He clicked on the heating as he passed the control, and entered the kitchen.

Nothing. No coffee dripping through the machine, no Jenna supervising it, not even any daylight yet.

He went to the front door and saw it was locked, but the chain he had put on the previous night as they went to bed was no longer securing their door. She must have gone out for some reason. He unlocked the front door and stepped outside. Within seconds he was shivering, but he could see no sign of his wife. Although it would be unusual, he wondered if she had been unable to sleep, so had gone out for an early morning walk through the woods, her favourite place to be.

Just a few steps out onto the path in his slippers was far enough and he called her name. There was no response. He headed back inside, dithering with cold. After setting the coffee machine to drip, Steve went back upstairs. No shower this morning, just a speedy dressing in warm clothes so he could poke his head out of the door and look for her again. He knew when he confessed his panic about her not being there that she would laugh at him, but in the five years since they had been together she had never simply disappeared without telling him what she was doing first.

The house was now starting to warm up, and his instinct was to put on warm outer clothing and head for their favourite walk, dipping down through the woods towards the pond, round the other side and back up to come out just below the church. He was at a loss as to why she would have done it without scrawling on a piece of paper that she had gone for a walk. She frequently left notes for him on the thin white paper that was easy to grab from the paper tray on their printer, rather than disturb him when he was working to tell him she was going shopping, or walking. No note, no Jenna, no coffee, no warmth. Something felt very wrong.

He poured a coffee as the machine indicated it was now ready, and cradled the cup in his hands as he went out the kitchen door. This one still had the chain in place where he had secured it the previous night, indicating she hadn't gone out of the back door. He called her name again. Silence was the answer.

He didn't want to admit to being worried, but somebody as yet unidentified had already killed once. Then he began to feel a little angry that Jenna hadn't thought how concerned he would be in view of the present circumstances.

He placed his coffee on the kitchen table and returned to the bedroom. Maybe she had left a note on her bedside cabinet, or even on his, saying where she was. But there was nothing. He was starting to get a bad feeling, and he was scared.

He checked every room. The three bedrooms revealed nothing. The bathroom revealed only one toothbrush, his blue one, and he felt sick. Where had she gone that necessitated taking a toothbrush? You didn't have to clean your teeth during a walk in the woods. He exited the bathroom and returned to the bedroom. He opened her chest of drawers. Every drawer was empty.

'She's gone?' he asked himself quietly. 'Why, Jen? Have I done something wrong?' He checked her wardrobe. Only a couple of items were still hanging there.

He ran down the landing to Jenna's office and sat at her desk, staring at the white envelope with his name on the front. He turned it over to unseal it and stared at the heart drawn on the pointed end of the flap.

Steve felt completely out of his depth, with no idea of what was going on. He opened the envelope and smoothed out the sheet of paper. It was definitely Jenna's handwriting. And there was a lot of it.

In the top right-hand corner where senders put their address, Jenna had written one word. *Somewhere.*

Steve felt sick. Wherever she was, she clearly didn't want Steve to try to follow. 'Somewhere, Jenna? Where the hell is that supposed to be?' he shouted. His voice echoed around the high-ceilinged room. And was he so unapproachable as far as his wife was concerned, that she felt she couldn't discuss her problems with him? There had been no indication that she had issues, and they had become quite excited at the prospect of a baby in the near future thanks to proposed IVF treatment.

He knew he had to read on. It was a long letter, filling the entire side of A4 paper.

My darling Steve,

I have so much to tell you that will be so far out of your understanding, and I know it will hurt you deeply. The main thing I am going to say and stress is that I have loved you since the first day we met, and I will love you until the day I die. But I have to go. I am sure at some point over the next two days DI France will arrive to arrest me and I can't be here when that happens.

Marjorie was accurate in saying Lucie Barker was at our door. She wanted to speak to you, and she told me she was your daughter. Her mother was called Angela Goldsmith when you were together, and Angela walked away from you because she didn't want the church. She was pregnant with Lucie, but didn't know it at that time. You left Sheffield to do your training and she married Philip Barker.

Lucie wanted to speak with you before Mass, to tell you. I asked her not to because it would distract you from such an important Christmas service, and I persuaded her to hang around in the churchyard at the end of the service to speak with you then.

I came back to the vicarage and collected a large knife. I knew she wasn't good for us. She would have created all sorts of loyalty issues, and I knew if you discovered you already had a child it would put our own family plans on the back burner. I walked back through the churchyard and left my coat on a headstone. I waited, and she came to stand by Emily Rowbotham's grave. She heard me behind her and was starting to turn around when I slashed her neck. She fell instantly.

I went back to our home, with my coat now covering any blood I may have accidentally splashed on myself, but I didn't have time to change because you messaged me.

When I bent down to check her pulse I made sure I got some of her blood on me, quite legitimately.

I had to do it for us, my love, to preserve what we have, but I now believe Adam and Debra will work it out. So I am leaving. I will miss you always, my darling, but I am catching a plane from Manchester to Chicago at 13.15, and I have no idea where I will go after that. I will never contact you again, that wouldn't be fair, but know I love you with all my heart. It was Lucie who spoilt it for us.

People will ask where I am. Make up any story you like, but take no blame. Lucie was your daughter and you would have grown to love her, but all I could see was she would cause trouble between us. I couldn't let that happen. And I can't be sorry I did what I did.

My love always
Your Jenna xxx

Paperclipped to the bottom was a much smaller piece of the printer paper, ripped from a larger sheet. Again Jenna's handwriting covered it.

My love, I ask for kindness from you. Please throw this small note away as soon as you have read it. I need this from you, and I believe you will act in the way I am asking because we have loved each other from the start. Please, don't contact Adam France until after I land in Chicago, to give me chance to be away from any issues at the airport. I will live the rest of my life away from my family, which will be punishment enough, but also away from you. That is almost unbearable. I know you will have to hand the main letter to Adam, but it could be Thursday when you find it?

Always my love xxx

Steve read both letters through twice, then eased them into a plastic sleeve to preserve them. He felt as though he was going to vomit, but knew that would come later when the whole saga would be relived in his mind in front of the cross. He looked at his phone – just after 7am. He searched for a number and clicked on it.

'Adam? It's Steve. Listen carefully because you need to act quickly. I have in my hands a confession from my wife to the murder of my daughter. She has left at some point during the night for Manchester airport where she is leaving on a plane bound for Chicago at 13:15.'

THE END

ALSO BY ANITA WALLER

Psychological thrillers

Beautiful

Angel

34 Days

Strategy

Captor

Game Players

Malignant

Liars (co-written with Patricia Dixon)

Gamble

Epitaph

Nine Lives

One Hot Summer

The Family at No. 12

The Couple across the Street

The Missing Ones

The House of Lies

Kat and Mouse series

Murder Undeniable (Book 1)

Murder Unexpected (Book 2)

Murder Unearthed (Book 3)

Murder Untimely (Book 4)

Epitaph

Murder Unjoyful (Book 5)

Supernatural

Winterscroft

The Connection Trilogy

Blood Red

Code Blue

Mortal Green

The Forrester Detective Agency Series

Fatal Secrets

Fatal Lies

Fatal Endings

ACKNOWLEDGEMENTS

My special thanks go to Betsy Reavley, who put the idea of a Christmas themed book into my head, and I loved writing it!

There is a team behind me who definitely are all deserving of a mention – Fred Freeman, Betsy Reavley, Tara Lyons, Abbie Rutherford, and Shirley Khan. Thank you for your support at all times, you are a pleasure to work with.

My beta readers and my ARC group also need a shout-out. Thank you for your support and encouragement over the last ten years, you're all special people.

I have two special friends who are my soulmates as we battle against editors, Amazon, and anybody else who upsets us, but we usually manage to sort it all out between us – Judith Baker and Valerie Keogh, thank you for being sensible, and sometimes crazy.

And finally I have to say thank you to all my family. I well remember one Saturday afternoon having a cup of tea on my Kirsty's patio, sharing the time with fourteen-year-old Lyra and ten-year-old Isaac, discussing the pros and cons of murder – who to kill, and who could be a potential killer. This book is the end result of that conversation.

The support of my family and friends since *Beautiful* was published in 2015 has been magnificent, and I thank you all from the bottom of my heart.

Anita Waller

June 2025

A NOTE FROM THE PUBLISHER

Thank you for reading this book. If you enjoyed it please do consider leaving a review on Amazon to help others find it too.

We hate typos. All of our books have been rigorously edited and proofread, but sometimes mistakes do slip through. If you have spotted a typo, please do let us know and we can get it amended within hours.

info@bloodhoundbooks.com